THE HIPPOGRIFF OF THE BASKERVILLES

Don D'Ammassa

Managansett Press Edition 2016

Wanda Coyne has solved the mystery of *The Maltese Gargoyle* and life has returned to its normal boring grind until a visitor tells her the intriguing story of the Baskerville family curse. With the help of her trustworthy assistant, Perry Everdeen, she has to discover whether Charles Baskerville met his death through natural or supernatural means, and protect his nephew and heir from sharing the same fate.

MANAGANSETT PRESS

Don D'Ammassa is the author of:

Horror
Blood Beast
Servant of Chaos*
Caverns of Chaos*
Wings over Manhattan
The Gargoyle
That Way Madness Lies*
Little Evils*
Passing Death*
Date with the Dark*
The Devil Is in the Details*
Living Things*
Shadows Over R'Lyeh*

Science Fiction
Scarab*
Haven*
Narcissus*
Translation Station
The Sinking Island*
Alien & Otherwise*
Wormdance*
Sandcastles*
Carbon Copies*
Phantom of the Space Opera*

Mysteries
Murder in Silverplate*
Dead of Winter*
Death at the Art Gallery*
Death on the Mountain*
Death on Black Island*

Fantasy
The Kaleidoscope*
Elaborate Lies*
The Maltese Gargoyle*
Perilous Pursuits*
Multiplicity*

Nonfiction
The Encyclopedia of Science Fiction
The Encyclopedia of Fantasy and
Horror
The Encyclopedia of Adventure Fiction
Masters of Detection Vol I*
Masters of Detection Vol II*
Masters of Detection Vol III*
Architects of Tomorrow Vol I*

*published by Managansett Press

THE HIPPOGRIFF
OF THE
BASKERVILLES

CHAPTER ONE

I suppose I should begin this account by identifying myself and presenting my credentials, as it were, for setting down what follows. My name is Perry Everdeen and for the last four years I have worked as private secretary, receptionist, researcher, and errand boy for Wanda Coyne, whom I believe to be the greatest detective in the city of Boston, if not the entire country. During that period I have, I think, earned and received the trust and confidence of my employer, who is admittedly a very difficult person to know well. She instructed me to call her Wanda from my very first day of employment, but I could tell even then that this was not an indication that she welcomed familiarity.

Wanda works alone for the most part. She might employ temporary subordinate to perform routine surveillance or send me to the library to research one subject or another, but she keeps her own counsel and types up her own summaries of each case. These are confidential for the protection of our clients, of course, but after the first few months of our relationship she indicated that I should familiarize myself with them at least in general terms. I have attempted to do so but I must admit that her style is terse and sometimes cryptic. She has a phenomenal memory and there was usually little more than an outline in those files. I am obviously much more knowledgeable about cases she has taken since I came to work for her, but even in those instances there are puzzling details which I will probably never understand.

Her most recent case – dare I refer to it as "our" case? – was a decided variation from her usual methods. I don't flatter myself that she thought I could contribute anything positive to the investigation, but it was necessary for her plans that she have a partner on the scene, and I was the logical choice. If I contributed anything at all rather than just serve as a kind of placeholder, then it was by chance or through her manipulation rather than because of any of my own qualities. I am pleased, however, that at the conclusion of our investigation, she indicated that I should be responsible for the case file. "There may be repercussions from these events in the future. I don't have the patience to complete the kind of detailed narrative that might be required. Since you were privy to most of the critical information and witness to several events where I was absent, why don't you write up the account from your point of view and I will add anything significant which you might have overlooked." And that very day I went to work.

Our first hint that we had a new client was the staff we found leaning against the office door on the morning of the fourth of May. Wanda's hours vary depending upon her caseload but I almost invariably arrived shortly before eight in the morning. It was rare but not unusual for us to reach the building simultaneously and this particular day was one of those exceptions. We rode up together in the levitator, having nodded greetings to each other. Neither of us was much inclined for conversation until we had coffee in our systems, and I'd been too rushed that morning to even think about brewing a pot. My wife was away for at least several weeks visiting her family – her mother lived alone and had just undergone necromantic surgery to remove a tumor - and my bachelor skills had atrophied very thoroughly. I was used to having breakfast waiting for me when I got up – Julia was traditionally domestic and rarely allowed me in the kitchen – and I'd had a restless night and had mildly overslept. As usual, Wanda had the morning paper rolled up in one hand.

The staff was propped up against our door and even from a distance we could see that there were runes carved along its length. We both stopped a few steps away and contemplated it for a few seconds. It is not wise to approach a wizard's staff even when no one is holding it. After a moment or two of silent observation, Wanda spoke to me without looking in my direction.

"We've had a visitor," she remarked blandly. "Although he has absented himself momentarily."

"Might be a woman," I ventured.

"No. The headpiece is carved so that it spirals clockwise. It's configured for a male. A woman's would be counterclockwise."

I hadn't known that, but then again, I've never spent much time studying the nuances of magic working, since I have no such talents of my own. I was not completely ignorant, however. "I see a caduceus. Isn't that the sign of a healer?"

"Yes it is. So our absent visitor has some connection to the medical profession."

I peered closer without approaching the staff. "I can see nicks and scratches. I'd guess that it's at least several years old, maybe decades. That suggests that its owner is no spring chicken."

"Unless it has been passed down from one generation to the next, or from a senior partner to a junior."

"I thought each person's staff had to be cut and inscribed to them personally."

Wanda nodded. "That is normally the case. Using another person's staff or wand involves a certain degree of risk. There are some cases where individuals who are particularly close have similar auras. I wouldn't rule the possibility out, but I agree that we're probably looking for someone who has been magically active for a long time."

"Where do you suppose he's gone?"

"Not far. I don't think our visitor is so elderly that he would forget his staff or deliberately leave it behind if he was going to be gone for long. Let's go inside and wait for him to return."

I eyed the staff warily. "Do you think it's safe?"

"I imagine so. If it was meant to harm us, it would have been concealed in some fashion. If its purpose is to keep us out of the office without harming us, there would be some indication of its intentions to warn us off. But I can unlock the door if you're worried…"

"No, I'll do it." I was not as confident as she was that no danger was involved, but I was determined not to disappoint her with a display of cowardice. I watched the staff warily as I made my way to the door and invoked the unlocking charm, but nothing untoward happened. Wanda followed me inside.

"I hope no one decides to steal it." I regretted my words immediately. The staff would be just a length of weathered wood in the hands of anyone but its owner. No one would bother to steal it. I covered my error by turning on the Never Empty Coffee Pot that Wanda had asked me to purchase recently. I had to admit that it was convenient – it never needed to be washed or refilled – but I didn't think it tasted as good as the coffee I'd brewed more mundanely in the past. I don't think Wanda actually ever tasted coffee though. She just needed the caffeine to kick start her metabolism.

Wanda had retreated to her private office so I brought her a cup – black and steaming. "Any signs of life out there?"

"Nothing yet." Two people had walked by the door, which was transparent glass, but neither of them had even looked my way. "I don't even know what I should be looking for."

Wanda's face was expressionless. "An older man, as we already deduced, with a receding hairline, glasses, and a scar on the back of his left hand. He'll be dressed conservatively, probably with a heavy cloak, and will have a New York City accent, although he no longer lives there. There will be dog hairs on his pants, I think, and he will be a bit out of breath."

Now I know that some private investigators have at least rudimentary powers of clairvoyance or spellcasting, but like me, Wanda is incapable of originating any form of magic. We can use charms prepared by others who do have those abilities, of course, but that's as far as we can go. And even if Wanda had purchased a Talisman of Seeing – which was unlikely given how expensive they were – she would never have expended its single usage on such a trivial matter. And even if she had, it would have required physical contact with the staff to enable her to obtain such a detailed picture of its owner.

"You're making that up."

"Not at all." Her face did not change expression, but I saw a hint of laughter in her eyes. "You see but you do not observe."

I turned my head, half expecting to see our mysterious visitor standing behind me, but the outer office was still empty. "There's something you're not telling me."

A brief smile came and went. "I'm afraid I am teasing you a bit. Look at this." She had unrolled the newspaper and it lay, mostly flat, on her desk as she turned it around. An older man with a high forehead, wearing slightly worn but expensive clothing including a heavy cloak, was seen alighting from a train. He wore glasses and one hand was raised, pointing out his luggage to a porter, and there was a dark line on the back, obviously an old but substantial scar. In his other hand, he held a staff that looked very much like the one that now rested against the outer wall of our office.

"What about the dog hairs?" I asked.

9

"The accompanying story indicates that Dr. Mortimer James has recently arrived in Boston. Dr. James was instrumental in the development of the first anti-diabetes spell when he was a much younger man. He surprised everyone at the time by choosing to retire early and live off the royalties, amusing himself with his longtime hobby, dog breeding, although I believe he also runs a small clinic. His strain of hellhound is particularly sought after by security firms. I recall that he maintains a kennel somewhere in northern Vermont."

"Why has he come to Boston?"

Wanda shrugged. "We'll have to ask him when he shows up."

And so he did, even as I was walking back to my desk. I saw him appear outside the door and recognized him immediately from the picture. James was even wearing the same clothing. He stooped to retrieve his staff and opened the door. I'm pretty good at reading body language and I could tell right away that he was agitated, although he had himself under control.

"There you are. I forget how late people sleep in the city." His voice was deep, resonant, and it was obvious even to me that he had lived in Brooklyn for a good part of his life. "I imagine it must have puzzled you to discover this," he raised his staff, "greeting your arrival."

Wanda came out to join us, extending her hand toward our visitor. "Not at all, Dr. James. I assume you left it to await our return and summon you from the coffee shop in the lobby. How was the cheese Danish this morning."

James looked briefly startled, then pleased. "I would wager that you recognized me from that horrible picture in this morning's newspaper. I can't imagine that they found me photogenic and I'm hardly famous enough to merit that much attention, so I would guess that there hasn't been much news of note lately."

"It has been a quiet spring. That's not necessary a bad thing, although in my line of business a little turmoil is not unwelcome."

"You are correct about the reason I left my staff as well. We have been together for so many years that it has become an extension of my consciousness. Since I had no idea when to expect you – you really should post your hours on the door – I decided to make myself comfortable while I waited and the breakfast at the hotel where I am staying was somewhat less than satisfactory. But however did you know what I had to eat?"

Since even I could see and interpret the smear of cheese on the edge of his cloak, Wanda's insight was not as surprising as it might have been.

"I have need of your services," said James at last. "Or at the minimum a consultation."

"Come into my office and we'll talk about it."

I was not present during this conversation and Wanda had closed the door. This was standard procedure and was designed to instill in our clients confidence that what they had to say was confidential. That was the truth, but Wanda sometimes discussed her cases with me quite frankly, using me as a sounding board, and while my duties were officially clerical, there were also times when I acted as a kind of apprentice investigator. I had no real ambitions in that direction, actually, but it was rewarding to know that Wanda trusted me not to embarrass her. And naturally I had access to all of her files,

In this particular instance, she took notes of their conversation which enabled me to reconstruct it after the fact. What follows may not be the exact words but it captures the essence of what passed between them, and Wanda herself has reviewed the text and pronounced it accurate.

Immediately upon sitting, James reached into an interior pocket in his cloak and extracted a scroll. Wanda could tell right away that it was not a modern artifact. Although incantations and such were ordinarily kept in bound books, the scroll had survived for its ornamental and ceremonial attributes. The Chief Magus of the Supreme Court was sworn in using a scroll that was nearly five centuries old – it was kept in a stasis sphere when not in actual use – and many organizations would inscribe their bylaws on a scroll even though for everyday use, pamphlets or other printed forms were more practical.

Modern scrolls used plastic rollers for the most part, although the fancier ones were arrayed on cast metal. The one that James carried had wooden rollers with elaborately carved headpieces and footers. They showed signs of wear and the small swathe of parchment visible had yellowed appreciably.

"That looks like a valuable artifact," said Wanda. "From the style of the carving, I would estimate at least two centuries."

"You have an educated eye, indeed. It dates from 1642 and has been a part of the Baskerville family tradition ever since. I am the first person outside the family to have it in my possession insofar as I know. It was entrusted to me by my dear friend, Charles Baskerville, shortly before his death this past winter."

Dr. James handed the scroll to Wanda, who carefully unrolled it on her desk. It was quite short and she was able to reveal the entire contents at once. The text had been inscribed by a quill pen and the handwriting and spelling were equally eccentric.

"The language is somewhat archaic and formal," continued James, "but I believe you will be able to follow the sense of it."

And so Wanda read the Baskerville scroll. I regret that I cannot reproduce the actual text as it was warded so that any attempt to copy it would result in a flawed version – a necessary precaution given its content, but Wanda summarized it to me later that same day.

It referred to an ancient curse that had afflicted the Baskerville family dating back at least three centuries. An ancestor named Hugo Baskerville had been lord of a moderately large estate somewhere in the north of England and he enjoyed a particularly foul reputation. Two wives had died at his hands, for he was a cruel man and subject to ungovernable rages. Their deaths were characterized as accidents, but no one believed his versions of events, for he was known as a great liar, prone to debauchery, crimes of various sorts, and murder. It was certain that he was a smuggler but he paid off investigators sent by the King or had their throats cut if they proved to be of a more honest disposition.

Hugo's favorite occupation was hunting, and he had trained a raptor –a griffin in fact - to spot his prey, then perch on his shoulder as he rode it down. Rumor has it that from time to time he hunted two legged animals as well, but he was so feared in that part of the country that he was never taken to task for his crimes. Hugo remained unmarried after the death of his second wife – there was a male son by the first wife who was raised by a governess and who almost never saw his father – and it seems that he must have been a lonely man because there is no indication that he ever formed a friendship, not even with his closest cronies, and spent most of his time keeping his own company.

He was not entirely alone, perhaps, because he exhibited a great fondness for the bird of prey, a mare that he had personally helped birth and rode almost exclusively, and a mongrel dog he had raised from a pup, a vicious animal who would allow no hand but that of his master to touch him. The raptor kept to a perch in Hugo's bedroom and the dog slept at the foot of his bed. It was said that he would have stabled the mare there as well if it had been practical.

Hugo never remarried after his second wife died, but that didn't mean that he was celibate. His tenants were in fact resigned to his occasional visits, during which he would mark which of their daughters was destined for his bed. When the mood struck him, he would send some of his retainers to forcibly remove the chosen maiden from her home and carry her off to his stronghold. Most would return the next day, walking disconsolately and alone. A few took their own lives. There is no record of any serious resistance because Hugo kept a well paid contingent of armed blackguards to enforce his will.

This went on for several years before one fateful day when Hugo gathered some of his minions and went hunting. The prey was supposed to be a fox but as it happened one of the village children, a ten year old girl, had wandered into the forest hunting berries. Hugo's dog was running ahead of the mounted party and for some reason he attacked the girl, perhaps because she had inadvertently crossed the fox's spoor. She was horribly mauled before Hugo called him off and she died of her injuries a few days later.

The girl's father carried the torn body up to the gates of Baskerville's stronghold, demanding to see Hugo, but he was denied entry. A few days later the dog was killed while out hunting on its own, stabbed multiple times and beheaded. The bereaved father refused to deny that he had killed the dog and everyone expected Hugo to have him beaten and driven off his land, or even killed. But Hugo's revenge was much crueler than that. The tenant had two other children, a son in his early teens, and a daughter who was old enough to have caught Hugo's eye. He had them both taken along with their father, who was forced to watch as they staked out the son so that Hugo could ride his mare back and forth over the prone body until it no longer looked human. And then he set his raptor on the girl and she died as well. The father was beaten but left alive to agonize over his lost children. He promptly disappeared.

13

Some weeks later, Hugo's mare was found butchered in its stall. The head and part of the torso were all that remained, the bulk of the body having been carried off in some fashion. Hugo was convinced that he knew who was responsible and he and his men combed the woods, searching for the one-time tenant. At some point Hugo sent his raptor aloft, but for the first time it failed to return. No trace of the bird was ever found.

Almost a year passed. Hugo was thrown from his new mount – or perhaps simply fell off in a drunken stupor for he had been drinking far more than ever. When the horse returned without its rider, his retainers organized a search party. They found his body on the very spot where the young girl had been savaged by the dog. His limbs and torso showed the imprint of a horse's hooves and almost every bone in his body was broken. The head was untouched, except that something sharp had been used to gouge on both of his eyes.

There was a large upright sheet of rock nearby and someone had used Hugo's own blood to inscribe a curse on the Baskerville family such that all of his male descendants would be watched over by the hippogriff, the union of raptor and mare, and if they were judged to be unworthy, the wrath that fell upon Hugo would be repeated for so long as the Baskerville line continued.

CHAPTER TWO

"Family curses are almost always spurious," said Wanda when she had finished reading. "And in those rare cases where they are genuine, a spell of Lineal Discontinuance is always almost effective in bringing one to an end."

"The Baskervilles resorted to that very procedure before some of them emigrated to America a century ago. The head of the family at that time, Simon Baskerville, did not entirely believe in the curse but there had in fact been some unexplained deaths during the intervening generations and he was persuaded that it would do no harm to take precautions."

"That was probably prudent, but there is another problem. There are no hippogriffs. There are griffins and horses, of course, just as there are trolls and unicorns, but the hippogriff is a myth along with gargoyles and vampires."

"There have been sightings."

Wanda dismissed the idea quickly. "Fabrications or illusions. It is possible to construct an inanimate creature and through magic give it the semblance of life. I've had a gargoyle fly around my apartment, as a matter of fact. But these are nothing more than clever mechanisms with magic as their source of power. They can only act as designed and unless their creator renews the spell that gives them the illusion of life, they will eventually return to their original lifeless state. Even if that ancient enemy of the Baskerville family was able to create some magical illusion to dispose of Hugo, it would long since have ceased to be a threat to anyone. It is more likely that the wounds were faked to support the purported curse, but that they had a much more mundane explanation."

"I cannot dispute anything that you say. In fact, I am of much the same mind. There is no timeless hippogriff watching over the Baskerville clan to punish the unwary for their sins. But there is in fact something that hovers around that family, something dangerous and implacable."

Wanda reports that James seemed reluctant to explain further, even though he had initiated the conversation, so she prodded him lightly. "You said that Charles Baskerville died recently, I believe. Was there any connection between his death and this supposed curse?'

"Appearances would suggest that. The ambiguity of the circumstances involved is troublesome."

"Tell me about it."

"First, you should know that Charles was a good man. I was his friend so I am hardly unprejudiced, but he enjoyed a superior reputation and as far as I know had no personal enemies. The American branch of the family is well off, though not as wealthy as was once the case. They acquired title to an estate in the northern part of Vermont, just over three thousand acres, most of it in a valley which is presently dappled with farms. They lease most of this land out rather than manage it directly. The Manor house sits on higher ground overlooking the valley, about one third of which would have to be reclaimed at rather great expense before it could be devoted to agriculture. It consists primarily of bogs and ravines and other ground unsuited to crops."

"How would you characterize the relations between himself and his tenants?"

"Smooth as silk, I say with some confidence. He and his father were both generous men who did not begrudge others the fruits of their labors. The rent is adequate to maintain the Baskerville family though not luxuriously. They do, however, have a considerable investment portfolio which has grown slowly but steadily over the years, primarily because the earnings have been turned into principal."

"No scandals, dark rumors, or other difficulties?"

"None. Charles himself was my friend, but admittedly he was a rather dull fellow. He was neither adventurous nor avaricious, a widower who was no longer interested in the pleasures of the flesh. There were no children. He was in good health overall, though slightly overweight. I was treating him for high cholesterol and blood pressure, but neither were at alarming levels. Charles was not a heavy drinker, and he smoked only a pipe and at rare intervals. He would have benefited from a more regular program of exercise, but he ate a balanced diet and took reasonably precautions with his health. He was, after all, in his late fifties and had become somewhat indolent."

"Was his household extensive?"

"Quite the contrary. He kept only two servants full time, a married couple named Lionel. A local service did most of the

16

cleaning on a weekly basis. Several rooms were no longer being used so a cook and a butler were his only concessions to tradition. The Lionels have been with him for more than twenty years and their characters are impeccable."

James fell into a short reverie at this point and Wanda rolled up the scroll while he was gathering his thoughts. "I had been after him to exercise more and he was making some effort. After dinner each evening he would walk around the grounds for half an hour. I would have preferred something more vigorous but any progress at all was welcome. He had mentioned to Barry Lionel that he was contemplating spending the weekend in New York City, but he never expressed any specific reason for it and as far as I have been able to determine, no definite plans had been laid. I had grown a bit worried about him by this time. He had seemed preoccupied and nervous during my last two visits – I live at one end of the valley – and on both occasions had referred to the family curse. I told him that it was nonsense, of course, and suggested that he consult a seer if he wanted reassurance. That may have been the purpose of his proposed trip, although I have no reason to draw that conclusion."

"Had anything unusual happened recently that might have preyed on his mind? A run of bad luck, a death in the area, anything of that sort?"

"Nothing of which I am aware. I have since talked to the Lionels and while they remain loyal to their employer even following his death, they admitted that he had been acting strangely lately. On one occasion he had reported seeing hoof prints in the garden, but when Lionel had investigated, he had found nothing amiss. On another he told Mrs. Lionel that he had found a coarse feather of considerable length lying on his bed, that he had put it aside to be investigated in the morning, and that it had disappeared from his dresser while he slept. On each of these occasions he had seemed unreasonably distraught and there had been an underlying feeling of tension in the Manor for several weeks. I witnessed this more pointedly during my last visit to the house while Charles was still alive. He was distracted and had trouble conversing, his blood pressure was as high as I had ever measured it, and he mentioned having recently revised his will to add some minor gifts to charities he favored. I told him that he was still a young man and that the charities would just have to survive without benefit of his largesse for another decade or two, but he smiled wanly and changed the subject."

"I don't mean to sound callous," said Wanda. "But isn't it possible that your friend was of unsound mind?"

"I considered that possibility of course, but it seems unlikely to me. All of the Baskervilles have been strong minded and there is no history of any mental disease in the family. Charles' health otherwise was not alarming. The onset of his mania was so sudden that I was worried about an undetected stroke or cancer of the brain, but he showed no other symptoms and willingly agreed to submit to a diagnostician specializing in that sort of disorder. He pronounced Charles to be free of any physical defect."

"What about arcane intervention? The family curse might have provided the framework for an attack by a more contemporary enemy. Someone could have cast spells of illusion that conformed to the legend."

James shook his head. "There is another factor which I have not yet mentioned. The Baskervilles have a long tradition of avoiding anything magical. There were rumors of black magic a few generations back, just before the move to America in fact, but no one was ever prosecuted. Charles, like his father, strongly objected to the practice and refused to make use of even simple charms or wards except under extreme circumstances. I was only allowed to prescribe herbal cures and other medicines when Charles was ill and in fact it took some persuasion to convince him to see a specialist. More importantly, the Manor and the grounds immediately surrounding are blanketed by a very powerful suppressive spell. No magic of any kind will function within the perimeter. Guests are warned in advance that any mystical palliatives or devices they might ordinarily rely upon will not function on the property. One can walk beyond its influence, of course, but this can be very inconvenient if the weather is unpleasant."

"Suppressive spells can be broken," Wanda pointed out.

"Yes, but not without leaving evidence of that intervention behind. There has been no such breach at Baskerville Manor. If hippogriffs were natural animals and existed, one could certainly have entered the grounds, but I agree with your assessment that they are creatures of myth that could only be simulated magically. And such a creation would become inert the moment it came into close proximity to the Manor."

Wanda confided to me that she was convinced that Dr. James was not telling her the whole story at this point, but conceded that he was probably not in a position to know the relevant details. "How exactly did Charles Baskerville die?"

"It was during one of his evening walks." James drew a deep breath. "He never ventured beyond the protective wards. If it was still light out, he usually walked in the gardens for about an hour. It was quite cold and overcast on the night in question, and it appears that he chose to cross behind the tennis court and follow a low stone wall that meandered down to the driveway. He could then follow the driveway back to the front door, or visit a small family cemetery surrounded by a thick grove of trees, but on the night in question he never made it that far. He died within a few meters of the graveyard."

James lapsed into a thoughtful silence for a few seconds before resuming. "Lionel became somewhat concerned when his master failed to return. It was cold, as I said, and Charles usually foreshortened his walks when the weather was bad. Lionel took a lantern and began to search the grounds, and found him almost immediately. Charles was lying about twenty yards from the driveway, face down. Lionel thought that he had fainted and carried him inside where he attempted to revive him while his wife called me. I went over immediately, of course, but there was nothing to be done, even if I'd been able to call upon my store of magical curatives. I would have suspected a simple stroke if it hadn't been for the marks. There were several deep cuts on his forehead and cheeks, the kind that might have been made by the claws of a griffin or other raptor."

"Was that the cause of death?"

"No. They would undoubtedly have been painful but they were not particularly serious. The body was sent for a scryopsy the following morning, but the results were inconclusive. His heart stopped, which was the immediate cause of death, but there was nothing to indicate why he should have experienced such a severe attack."

"Did the authorities investigate at all?"

"There was a cursory inquiry. There were at least three odd circumstances, none of which seemed to interest Detective Raines particularly. A griffin feather was found caught in a privet hedge close to where Charles fell. And a few feet away, there were faint hoof prints – barely visible given that the ground was nearly frozen – as though a horse or unicorn had passed by."

"The feather might have blown there," suggested Wanda.

"That's what Raines said. It was a damned coincidence if true, but I saw no purpose in arguing the point. And the hoof prints might have been there for several days, according to him. Technically, I suppose that he was right, but the Baskervilles don't keep livestock except for housecats and sometimes dogs. The prints were inside the gated area of the property, so could not have been left by some passing equestrian. Raines admitted that it was a mystery, but could see no relevance to his investigation. And so the matter ended. I had no grounds to insist upon a more sophisticated examination of the circumstances."

"You said that there were three anomalies."

"Yes, but the third is hard to describe. It appears that Charles lingered near the end of the stone wall for several minutes, then turned and tiptoed across a stretch of disturbed ground and onto the grass."

"Tiptoed?"

"There were only a few prints, but none of the heel."

"Was it proven that they were his?"

"Oh, yes. They matched his shoes perfectly and some of the dirt had adhered to the soles."

Wanda told me later that she suspected at this point that there was a simple explanation to at least part of the mystery. It was entirely possible that James was dramatizing what was, after all, a rather mundane situation, although with some baroque embellishments. It was most likely that Charles Baskerville had indeed died of a stroke, perhaps provoked by his unhealthy obsession with the family curse. Something had happened during his evening walk that had triggered that violent and fatal reaction, perhaps simply an overactive imagination. Griffins were not unknown in northern New England, although they preferred warmer climates, and it was possible that one had alighted near Baskerville and startled him so violently that it had resulted in his death.

Griffins, being natural creatures, would not have been affected by the magical ward. The hoof prints could be explained in many ways. Dr. James was not part of the Baskerville household and it was conceivable that Charles had entertained a mounted visitor or allowed a neighbor to ride across his property. The odd prints puzzled her not at all. Charles Baskerville had been running when he died, perhaps from a stray griffin who had been provoked into attacking.

"How far was the body from the terminal point of the warding spell?"

James considered this for a moment. "Perhaps thirty yards. It generates a hemisphere originating inside the house and encompasses the fenced yard and gardens, the cemetery, the driveway almost as far as the larger front gate."

"Is that gate secured at night?"

"It is kept closed but has never been locked to my knowledge. Charles liked and trusted his neighbors. In any case, it would have been easy to circumvent on foot or horseback. A vehicle would have been barred, however, because the property is heavily wooded."

"Were there any visitors at the Manor that night?"

"None. Nor had there been for several days except tradesmen making deliveries."

"Were the hoof prints on a paved surface or the lawn?"

"Neither, actually. The driveway is gravel and would not have shown anything. There was a strip of bare earth, however, which had been dug up in anticipation of a new stretch of privet, but the planting had been deferred until the spring. That's where the prints were visible, running parallel to the driveway for about ten paces before they disappeared."

Wanda fell silent, but Dr. James perked up. "There's one thing I forgot to mention, although I don't know if it is important."

"Anything might help."

"I'm quite sure that Charles had been standing near the wall for at least several minutes before he started across the lawn and died. Detective Raines agreed with my assessment but deemed it unimportant."

"How exactly did you determine that?"

"Charles had taken his pipe and when I looked at it, I noticed that he had finished at least half of a plug."

"He might have done that at any point."

James looked quite smug as he explained. "I am not completely unobservant. I also found a discarded dottle lying not far from the wall. He had obviously cleaned his pipe and refilled it, then smoked for a considerable period of time before his death."

"An astute observation, Dr. James. I don't see how it moves us forward specifically, but every new fact nudges us that much closer to a solution."

"Most healers have trained themselves to be observant."

"And I take it that there were no indications that he had not entertained a visitor. A human visitor, that is."

"None whatsoever, or at least none that could be detected. As I mentioned, the grass was nearly frozen and the driveway was gravel. There are no close neighbors and the tree cover is quite thick. One could have lit a small bonfire without attracting any attention except from the Manor itself. The passing road is infrequently travelled, and snow had been forecast, though none fell. The police were unable to find any local resident who might have seen strangers or anything unusual that evening."

"You must have some theory, Mr. James. I doubt that you came all this way just to tell me a ghost story."

"I am a man of science as well as magic, Miss Coyne. I am convinced of the effectiveness of the warding spell and am confident that it was not subverted. When you eliminate the supernatural, then only the rational remains. I believe that Charles Baskerville was murdered by someone using devilishly clever tactics. The police are not interesting in expensive and time consuming investigations and they prefer to believe that natural causes are the explanation. It is my understanding that you have shown a certain skill at ferreting out the truth when more traditional investigators have thrown up their hands. I would like to hire your services to determine the truth."

"I am only licensed within the Commonwealth of Massachusetts."

"There is nothing to prevent a private citizen from pursuing a personal whim, is there? There is no ongoing police investigation so you would not be interfering with the authorities."

Wanda was of two minds. The mystery did intrigue her mildly, although she thought that the police might well have made the proper determination. And we only had two open cases at the time.

One of those was a routine surveillance job that she had already farmed out to one of her subcontractors and the other was likely to be tied up within twenty-four hours, a missing person whom we had almost certainly located in Atlanta. On the other hand, she was at her best in her present environment. She had grown up in a very rural community in the western part of the state and had fled to the city as soon as she was old enough to be independent. And she rarely ventured beyond the suburbs.

I suspect she had fallen into a brief reverie to wrestle with these thoughts when James stirred uncomfortably. "There is something more I should tell you. There have been other incidents which I am not totally able to dismiss."

"What sort of incident?"

"One of the tenant farmers heard a disturbance two nights before Charles died. He ventured out into the darkness to investigate with a flashlight, but he expected nothing worse than a stray dog and was not armed. He insists that he saw a large animal passing through a freshly tilled field. Initially he thought that someone's horse was loose – there are several people in the valley who keep them – and his first thought was to take it by the mane and try to return it to its owner. But when he approached, the animal turned its head and the farmer – John Turner – insists that it was the head of a griffin and that it was clearly aroused. He stumbled backward and fell, momentarily dropping the flashlight. When he recovered, it was cantering away toward the head of the valley. He made no attempt to follow it but returned and told the story to his wife, who remained skeptical even though he showed her the tracks the following morning. He made a belated attempt to follow them by daylight, but they disappeared when they reached the road that runs behind his farm."

"It is easy to be mistaken in the darkness, particularly when startled."

James nodded. "Such was my conclusion when I first heard the story. But he also mentioned that the eyes glowed red like those of the Kandahar Demon at the National Zoo. And there were two more sightings – both at a considerable distance but by individuals whose characters I would say were reliable. In the first instance, a young couple who run a convenience store in the village center were driving back home the following night when they saw what they assumed was a late night rider galloping along an elevated footpath that parallels the road. They were concerned because there are no lights there and the going is treacherous in spots, so the wife was watching closely as they passed. She suddenly cried out and grabbed at her husband's arm so violently that he pulled off to the side of the road. She was quite insistent that the horse – or whatever it was – had turned to look down at them and that it had the face of a devil with glowing eyes."

"Did she see anyone riding this creature?"

"No, but she insisted that there was some kind of shape rising above its shoulders. She thought it looked like enormous furled wings."

"If it is capable of flight, why would it risk a dangerous trail in the darkness?"

James shrugged. "It was indeed seen flying later that same night. Two young lads were larking about when they heard what they describe as the drumming of hooves approaching. They were on yet another footpath and had just passed an abandoned barn and they stepped off into the tall grass to allow the presumed rider to pass. The thundering of feet suddenly stopped and they were cautiously looking back the way they had come when something large and dark with glowing red eyes and threshing wings rose from behind the barn and flew rapidly off into the distance. Or so they say."

"Boys tend to be imaginative, and prone to pranks."

"Of course. And if it hadn't been for the prior sightings – and the subsequent tragedy – I would not have given their stories a second thought. But their parents insisted that the boys were genuinely upset and frightened when they arrived home, and they are both quite reliable in the ordinary course of things."

"So are you still convinced that there is a rational explanation?"

James shook his head. "Frankly, I don't know what to believe. The hippogriff does not exist. There is nothing in the fossil record to indicate that it ever did. I know that magic can be used to create hybrids from species that are not ordinarily interfertile, but they are invariably sterile and the procedure only succeeds when the subjects are relatively similar biologically. Necromancers have created alligators with rattles and a poisonous bite, and hummingbirds that have characteristics of a bird of prey, but a griffin and a horse are just too dissimilar."

Wanda stood up at this point and began pacing, which had I been present would have convinced me that she was indeed going to take the case – whatever the case was. Pacing was always a sign that she had made the transition from listening to considering. "Who stood to benefit from Charles' death?"

"Well, primarily his heir, Henry Baskerville, although there were more than a dozen smaller legacies. Charles had two brothers, Richard and Arthur. Richard returned to England while still a young man when it appeared that the family name was headed toward extinction there. He fathered Henry and a sister, the latter of whom died in infancy. Richard himself passed away well before his time after a hunting accident left him in a wheelchair. Arthur was something of a black sheep. He became interested in necromancy and went to Haiti to study voodoo.. Apparently he grew impatient with the reluctance of his mentor to reveal the secrets of his craft and attempted to make off with some powerful arcane object. He was found beheaded in a hotel room The head was never found, in fact, and that of a black sheep had been sewn onto the body in its place. He had taken a native wife, but there were apparently no children."

"Henry is therefore one of two nephews, the last of the Baskervilles. Charles himself was without children, unless he sired a bastard somewhere along the line. Unless Henry conceives a male child, the family name will end with this generation."

"Are you quite sure Arthur is dead?'

James nodded his head. "The evidence seems undeniable. The original scryopsy was confirmed when the body was returned. He's buried in the family cemetery at the Manor. I met him only once and when he was still a child. It didn't require precognition to predict that he would come to a bad end. I never met Richard. He had just left the country when I came to live in the valley. I know that he had returned to England intending to try to restore the original Baskerville Hall."

"And you have never met Henry either?"

"No, but as one of the administrators of the will, I cabled the authorities there and asked them to advise the Baskerville family of the situation. I knew very little about Henry at the time. Charles rarely mentioned him and had not even told me that his nephew had been knighted. Henry contacted me via empathic link and we have corresponded more conventionally since then. For a variety of reasons, it was impractical for him to leave England until now. He is flying into Boston later today and I am frankly unable to decide what to say to him."

"Have you advised the gentleman of the mysterious circumstances and your suspicions?"

"I have intimated that there are unresolved questions, but when I tried to reduce my fears to writing, I am afraid they seemed rather childish. Certainly I am unable to make a convincing case. Nevertheless, I have grave reservations about allowing Henry to stay at Baskerville Manor."

"Has there been any suggestion of danger to Henry specifically?"

James seemed more uncomfortable than ever. "No, nothing at all. There have been no further appearance of the hippogriff. But I have no idea what kind of man he is. If Charles – about whom I know little to his discredit – was found sufficiently lacking in character to cause the curse to fall upon him, then how can I feel confident that the same fate does not await his heir?"

"Then you do think that there is a supernatural cause?"

James shook his head in exasperation. "As I told you, I don't know what to think. I lack sufficient confidence in either explanation to make a decision, and I would feel terrible guilt if my actions – or lack of actions – resulted in another tragedy."

Still pacing, Wanda fell into a brief silence. "The curse does not seem to have constrained itself. First it was in England, then it appears to have followed the family across the ocean. I don't suppose Henry himself has had any experience of it?"

"I don't know. He says not. His mother died of cancer and his father as the result of an accident. That's all I know about their deaths. There doesn't appear to be any hint that anything unnatural was involved."

"And there is no reason to believe that the curse is limited to the grounds of Baskerville Manor, is there? These other incidents you mentioned all took place outside of the property, didn't they?"

"Yes. The boys were at the far northern end of the valley and the married couple was on the southern road."

"Then let us say that the curse is real, just for the sake of argument. Why couldn't it strike down Henry in England, or at a hotel outside the valley, or anywhere else if it wanted to? Presuming that he had committed some sin which left him vulnerable."

"I suppose that is true."

"Then there is no purpose to be served by convincing him not to stay at Baskerville Manor."

James considered. "Yes, I see that now. I hadn't thought of it that way."

"Then he's as safe there as anywhere else. But I suggest this. I assume you don't plan to drive up to Vermont this evening."

"No, of course not. We have rooms here in the city. I am sure Henry will be fatigued after the long flight. I had planned to drive back tomorrow."

"Might I suggest that you bring him here first. I may have some recommendations to make after I've considered the problem. I won't delay you long. You can tell him that I am examining the circumstances of Charles death and that this is completely informal"

"Very well. I shall do that very thing." James stood up. "I appreciate your patience in listening and taking seriously what may well be the excessive worries of a gullible old man."

"Nothing of the sort. I do have one last question though. Charles Baskerville has been dead for several weeks now."

"More than two months. Henry needed to put his affairs in order before he could leave England."

"Yes, well during that time, you said that there have been no further sightings of the hippogriff, or anything else unusual?"

"No sightings at all. But there wouldn't be, would there? There are no Baskervilles in residence."

"True. But have there been strangers about, or unusual thefts or vandalism, unexplained deaths of livestock, anything of that sort?"

"A number of policeman have been to the valley in connection with Charles' death. I suppose someone else could have misrepresented himself as one of them without my knowing about it. But otherwise, no, at least nothing that I am aware of. Is that significant?"

"Everything is potentially significant, even by its absence. I will see you tomorrow then?"

"Assuredly."

CHAPTER THREE

Wanda spent the rest of the morning in her office with the door closed, although I noted that she made at least two telephone calls herself rather than having me put them through. I left her undisturbed until well after noon, at which point I used the intercom to ask whether or not she wanted me to order something to eat.

"Not just yet. Don't wait for me; I operate on stored energy when I'm thinking."

"Are we taking Dr. James' case then?"

"I will decide that in the morning, after I meet Henry Baskerville. But he has brought us an interesting problem."

I had lunch in the coffee shop on the ground floor and took my time about it. At this point I was not familiar with the story related by our visitor and my thoughts were occupied by plans for a two week vacation that Wanda had promised me during the coming summer. Julia and I had sent away for various brochures but we were having trouble compromising on a location that would suit both our natures. I wanted someplace restful, even bucolic, where I could sit on a porch with a book, or nap beside a stream while pretending to fish, or if I was really feeling ambitious take an extended hike through a quiet stretch of forest. Julia preferred something a little more lively, or at least touristy, and preferred attending a druidic gala in the Luray Caverns, or riding unicorns at a dude ranch in Texas. Contrary to legend, virginity was not a requirement. This particular strain had been bred to tolerate sexually experienced riders.

Wanda's door was still closed when I returned, but she appeared a few minutes later, looking – not happy exactly – but less doleful. I noticed that the counter on the Never Empty Coffee Pot had increased by ten. This month's bill would be higher than usual. She was carrying a large piece of parchment which turned out to be a map.

"I had a courier deliver it while you were out," she explained. "Baskerville's valley and the surrounding area." She summarized what Dr. James had told her, leaving out much of the detail which I only learned later that day when she had me transcribe her handwritten notes. In fact even then I was missing a number of points which emerged piecemeal over the next few hours as she mentioned them, then explained when I looked puzzled.

Baskerville Manor was perched on a kind of ledge – artificial as it turned out – that overlooked the valley proper, which was wide in the middle and narrow at both the northern and southern ends. There was no obvious access from the east or west, where the terrain lines suggested impassible scarps and ravines. I would later learn that the area was even more impenetrable than it seemed because of the heavy overgrowth. The farms which Baskerville leased to his tenants made a patchwork quilt across most of the center of the valley, but the two ends were almost completely undeveloped. The southern region was largely swampland as the underground river that made agriculture possible bubbled to the surface in several places. A small village occupied the geographical center of the valley and the main road ran from north to south. The legend on the map identified the village as Grimalkin. The main road was paved but the subsidiary ones leading to the individual farms were not.

Baskerville Manor could almost have been a fortress in terms of placement. The main gate was at the roadway, flanked by lines of trees so thick that no vehicle could pass through them. This gate was ordinarily left open, but after another hundred yards there was a secondary gate, and this was closed at night, though not always locked. The driveway – which was gravel for its entire length – passed through this gate and meandered through two S curves before ending at the Manor. The grounds here were heavily populated with trees and shrubbery and there was a shoulder high stone wall around the house proper. A small private cemetery stood to one side of the house and a larger, formal garden wrapped its way from the opposite side and along most of the rear wall. There was a small pond which was almost certainly man made, and two outbuildings, one of them quite large. Fifty yards behind the Manor, the ground rose abruptly like a ragged stone wall and merged into the mountainous perimeter.

The map also included the area directly abutting the valley. A meandering structure to the north proved to be the Sebastian Adult Correctional Facility. The town of Moran was situated to the south. For the most part, however, the valley appeared to be surrounded by dense forest.

Wanda asked me what I thought of Dr. James' story, or at least of the truncated version she had provided. I asked how certain it was that the ward protecting the Manor from all magic could not be penetrated. "Assuming that it was put in place by a reputable sorcerer, and that the subsequent examination of its efficacy was competent, I'd agree with James. It would be impossible for it to have been breached undetectably."

"Then you believe there is a non-magical explanation?"

"I don't rule anything out. Arcane researchers are constantly discovering things that were previously unknown. The word 'impossible' has become more of a tendency than a fact. It is much too early to form any real opinion. But remember. Magical effects must have an organic source. Curses and charms and wards and such are all prepared by men or women. They do not spontaneously generate themselves."

"But unicorns and dragons have magic," I objected.

"They have magical attributes, but they have not created them. Creation requires a higher degree of intelligence."

I considered the problem. "But a magical artifact can survive the death of its creator. If this really is a family curse, it began generations ago and the originator is long dead."

Wanda nodded. "Which raises the question of why the curse chose to renew itself now, if that is what happened. By all reports, Charles Baskerville was not a particularly offensive man. What sin did he commit that was so horrible that it deserved death?"

"He may have had secrets about whose existence Dr. James had no hint."

"If that's the case, our job will be to discover them. Clearly the police are either incompetent or inattentive."

"How so?"

"They concluded that the dead man tiptoed across the lawn before his death. Ludicrous. The reason there were no marks of his heels was because he was running. Nor did they take particular note of the discarded dottle or the coincidence of the claw marks."

An image flashed across my mind, a man running in terror as a rampant hippogriff hovered above him. "But why was he running away from the house? If something frightened him, wouldn't he have sought safety indoors?"

Wanda's mouth twitched in what might have been a stillborn smile. "Good thinking, Perry. That was my thought exactly. It is possible, of course, that he was running toward something, but given the circumstances, he was almost certainly fleeing for his life. Ineffectually, as it turned out. And don't forget those claw marks – they are undoubtedly significant." She was suddenly thoughtful. "I wonder whether or not they were post mortem. I shall have to ask the good healer tomorrow."

"My question still stands. If he was attacked by something, natural or unnatural, why run away from his only hope of assistance?"

" I suspect that he was so terrified by whatever assailed him that he became disoriented. Whatever the truth really is, Charles Baskerville almost certainly believed that he was facing the wrath of the family curse. I am not at all surprised that his heart gave out. The question is whether or not he had misinterpreted some other phenomenon entirely – perhaps driven mad by remorse for some secret sin – or whether there was some unsuspected instrumentality involved, either a curse that manages to circumvent one of the basic laws of magic, or at the hands of some person who wanted him, and us, to believe that this was the case."

I mulled that over for a few seconds while Wanda began to pace again, this time in the outer office. "Didn't you say that your wife was away?"

"Yes I did. She's staying with her mother for a while, then visiting her siblings while she's on the West Coast."

"So you have nothing keeping you in Boston."

Puzzled, I admitted that I did not.

"Depending upon tomorrow's interview, I might suggest that we close up the office for a week or so and indulge ourselves with a field trip. You drive, don't you?"

I was licensed, but did not have an automobile, gasoline or ley powered.

"Then we may have to lease one. I can't do justice to this case from secondhand information. We may need to visit Vermont. Happily, the winter is over though I imagine it is still quite chilly that far north."

I didn't say anything. Wanda had never taken me out with her on a case before, although I sometimes ran errands connected to them. But then again, she had never worked a job that required her to be outside the city for more than a few hours, at least not since I had worked for her. This case had already become quite unusual.

It would continue this trend in the days that followed.

CHAPTER FOUR

Our two guests arrived promptly the following morning. I had come in a few minutes early but Wanda was already in her office and the Never Empty Coffee Pot was bubbling away already. Looking back over what I have already written, I notice that I never completely described Mortimer James. He was an older man, approaching sixty, with thinning hair that had mostly turned to silver grey. He was not a particularly tall man, for I had at least a couple of inches advantage at five foot eight. He was heavy in the shoulders and thighs and I suspected he had been active in his younger years but had allowed himself to gain more weight than was good for him. Given his profession, he must have known this but had apparently declined to resort to thinning potions. It was a case of healer physic thyself.

In contrast, his companion was taller, younger, and much more fit. I would have guessed – correctly – that he was still a few years shy of forty. His hair was dark and thick and it crowned reasonably handsome though perhaps slightly hard features. He was dressed expensively and carried himself with obvious assurance and the grace that came with an active life. He silently allowed his eyes to roam around the outer office in frank appraisal and, I suspect, a certain degree of disapproval. I wondered how much James had told him and how he had convinced the man of the wisdom of this visit. That question was answered for me a short time later and this time I was invited to remain in Wanda's office, seated on a small divan in one corner where I could take notes and surreptitiously watch our visitors from a position where they were not likely to invest any particular attention in me.

"I appreciate your patience in humoring my request for an interview," said Wanda to open the conversation.

"Not at all," replied Sir Henry Baskerville heartily. "In fact, something rather odd happened last night and I would appreciate a professional opinion."

James was looking quite subdued and, I thought, far more concerned than he had the day before. "We have had a communication," he said. "A most puzzling one."

Baskerville fumbled with the inside pocket of his jacket and extracted a folded piece of paper which he placed on the desk in front of him. "This message was left at the desk shortly after we checked in. There is no signature, as you can see."

Wanda picked up the paper and read it aloud, presumably for my benefit. "If you value your life, return to England immediately."

"It seems that my presence has offended someone," said Baskerville. "And how the deuce did the writer know where we were staying? We only decided after customs released my luggage and we didn't speak of it to anyone."

"Did you call to make a reservation?"

"No. We went straight from the terminal to the hotel. It was the Adler, down near the waterfront."

"Then it is likely that you were followed. Did you ask the desk clerk who left the message?"

"I certainly did, but it was apparently a random street urchin. He was unable to provide any useful description."

Wanda let the paper drop to the desk. "This hardly seems the kind of tactic one would associate with a family curse, Dr. James."

The healer bestirred himself. "No, of course not. It might however be a warning rather than a threat, sent by someone who believes in the Baskerville curse and thinks Henry might be in danger."

"Then why remain anonymous?"

James shrugged. "Many people prefer not to become involved in the difficulties of others."

"Perhaps." Wanda managed to express serious doubt in a single word. "But our unknown correspondent has gone to great lengths to ensure his or her anonymity. The individual words were all cut out of a newspaper and glued in place. Judging by the typeface, I'd guess it was not the Boston Globe. I will hold onto this for the present if I may. Do you have many acquaintances in this country, Sir Henry?"

"They are all gathered in this room," he replied shortly, but I noticed that he looked away from Wanda. It was patently a lie and I was sure that Wanda would have noted that fact.

"Then it probably was not the case that you would have recognized the handwriting. Or do you have correspondents here?"

"I have received occasional letters from business associates and the inevitable begging letters from charitable institutions. Nothing more."

Wanda glanced down at the letter. "Preparing this required some time and effort. When exactly did you arrive?"

Dr. James and Baskerville exchanged looks and James answered. "It was just a few minutes after six."

"And when did you receive the letter?"

"We dined in the hotel and passed the desk on our way back to our rooms. It would have been half past eight or thereabouts."

"And when was the message left at the desk?"

Another exchange of looks. "We didn't ask," said James.

"It doesn't matter. I would have said that this took a while to assemble. It is very neatly done and it probably took some time to find the word 'England' and 'immediately,' but of course the sender could have prepared it well in advance in anticipation of an opportunity to deliver it without revealing the author's identity."

"It's damned presumptuous if you ask me." Baskerville was openly indignant.

"Has anything else unusual occurred since your arrival?"

Baskerville mulled the question for a moment. "There is the matter of the missing shoe."

James shifted his weight. "That probably happened when the customs agent opened your bags, Henry. I thought at the time that he was unusually careless. It probably fell to the floor and was overlooked when we were passed through. I told you we could file a claim."

Baskerville shook his head impatiently. "Not worth the effort, Mortimer. I had bought them expressly for this trip, though. It's a shame not to have worn them even once."

Wanda leaned forward. "When exactly did you notice that it was missing?"

Baskerville folded his arms and sat back in his chair. "It was after we returned to our rooms. Because of the difference in time zones, I was starving by the time we reached the hotel. As soon as we were checked in, we went down to the dining room for what I might say was a disappointing meal. I was starting to flag by then so we had strong coffee afterwards and spent the better part of two hours downstairs. As you've already heard, we stopped at the desk on our way back and then separated. Mortimer's room is on the same floor but some distance from mine. I went inside and began to unpack, intending to make an early night of it. It was then that I discovered that I had an odd number of shoes."

"Was anything else missing?"

"I am not aware of anything, but my man back home did the packing for me and I cannot be certain."

"Was anything present that you were not expecting to find?"

"No, nothing at all. I really don't think any of this is important."

"And it may not be," agreed Wanda readily. "But assume for a moment that the customs agent was not careless."

"You mean he took my shoe deliberately? Whatever for?"

"I think that unlikely. But was your luggage locked while you were dining?"

Baskerville frowned. "No it wasn't. I opened two of the bags for a fresh shirt and handkerchief."

"Then someone might have absconded with your shoe while you were downstairs. I'm sure you did lock the door to your room, but there are charms that will disable all but the most sophisticated of locking spells, and the Adler is hardly the most modern hotel in Boston."

Baskerville absorbed that thoughtfully. "But why a single shoe? Or even a pair of them, for that matter."

"I suspect we will have the answer to that in time. It would be useless to speculate at present."

"I am forced to speculate, given the scarcity of actual facts to consider. What is this all about anyway?"

Wanda glanced at Dr. James, who sighed. "I didn't share my concerns with Henry last night. He was clearly fatigued by the trip and I thought it best to wait until this morning."

Baskerville glanced at him with, I thought, the slightest trace of hostility. "What is it that you've been withholding from me, Mortimer? Do I strike you as the sort who requires pampering?"

Wanda quickly interceded. "It was probably best that he waited so that we could all share our thoughts. Perhaps it would be best if the doctor were to recount the story that he told us yesterday. In complete detail if you would, sir."

James was squirming a bit, but he launched into his story and became more confident once he had begun. Baskerville listened intently and without interruption and as far as I could see the expression on his face remained unchanged throughout. James faltered toward the end and Wanda prompted him for some details which he had left out, and he hastily corrected himself. When he was finished, there was an uncomfortable, prolonged silence. It was Baskerville who finally spoke.

"It seems that my sudden good fortune has not come without its darker side. I was aware of the family curse, of course. My rather used to speak of it from time to time, but always disparagingly. There is even a painting of the hippogriff in the family seat, although I found it in the attic as a child and it has never been displayed during my lifetime. Father doubted that it had ever been more than a fable and assured me that hippogriffs were no more real than harpies or chimera. I think one of our ancestors had taken steps to reverse the curse, probably as a precaution rather than an actual response to a threat. In any case, it was not something that we took seriously. And now you tell me that in some form it may be responsible for the death of my uncle."

"It is possible that there is a more mundane human agency responsible," said Wanda. "If the note you received is a threat, it lends credence to that supposition."

"And if it's a warning, it may just be a well intentioned gesture by someone unacquainted with the actual facts of the matter."

"Precisely. The missing shoe, if it is related, poses more questions and no answers. But the immediate question, which we must answer now and with insufficient knowledge is whether or not you should travel to Baskerville Manor."

"You think I may be in danger then?"

"I'm afraid I don't know the answer to that question either, but certainly the possibility of danger exists. Charles Baskerville died of heart failure but it was not a natural death. He was frightened out of his wits and something had wounded him in the face. Whether natural or supernatural, his death was murder."

Baskerville straightened up in his chair. "There is no question as to whether or not I go to the Manor, Miss Coyne. I was brought up to believe that the Baskervilles were a proud family despite our reduced circumstances and I have made some progress in reversing that condition, as did my father before me. I will not be driven away by anonymous letters or hints of supernatural enmity. But neither am I a rash man. I believe that I will delay my departure," he glanced to James as if for permission, "one day further. I wish to purchase a few items here in the city which might not be as readily available in the countryside. I would be foolish not to take some elementary precautions."

James leaned forward. "I would be happy to defer our departure another day, Henry, but I should remind you that the Manor is warded. Nothing magical will function within the house or its immediate environs. Unless you choose to have the ward taken down, of course, but I would not recommend such a course until you have considered it at length."

Baskerville nodded. "Let it stay, at least for the time being. But I was thinking of more mundane forms of self protection. I am skilled with both long guns and pistols and I understand that Charles kept none."

"No, he was not fond of hunting or other blood sports."

"Well, imaginary or not, I can't imagine any creature short of an adult dragon impervious to a modern rifle." Baskerville sounded confident, but James clearly was not reassured.

Wanda seemed satisfied, however. "Then perhaps we could lunch with you at your hotel, at one o'clock?"

Baskerville nodded his assent. "But if you have more to tell us…"

"Not at the moment. I beg your indulgence for a few hours. My assistant and I," I suppressed a smile at my imaginary promotion, "will look into a few matters and report to you whatever might prove helpful."

"All right. I can be a patient man when it is in my own interests." Baskerville rose to his feet abruptly and James hastily followed suit. "I am pleased to have made your acquaintance and look forward to whatever you may have to tell us." He didn't include me in his expression of pleasure, but I was used to that.

I waited until I had shown them to the door before giving Wanda a quizzical look. "Your assistant?"

"A temporary promotion, and I need you in that roll immediately. Lock up the office. We must hurry."

We reached the lobby just as Baskerville and James were getting into a cab. Wanda restrained me with a hand on my arm until the cab pulled away, after which we hastened outside and she flagged another. "Would you be so kind as to follow that Centaur cab just ahead of us without making our interest obvious?"

The driver turned to look back at us. "This is a joke, right?"

Wanda handed him a large denomination bill. "It's no joke and we'll lose them if you don't hurry."

He hurried. We followed the cab, which headed straight downtown and stopped only a few minutes later, disgorging its passengers in front of a sporting goods store. Wanda told our driver to let us out a block short, paid him, and the two of us took advantage of a briskly moving crowd to keep our two clients under observation without being seen ourselves. But Wanda had noticed something that I had completely overlooked. The two men disappeared inside the shop and as they did so she indicated that we should cross to the same block. "Let's see if we can get a better look at our mystery man."

I had no idea what she was talking about and it must have shown in my face. "We weren't the only people following Sir Henry. Another cab, a Red Dragon, was parked across the street and it moved out right after Baskerville. Its passenger is now standing in the doorway of that office building on the corner where he can watch the entire block."

Our quarry was standing in shadows and all I could determine was that he was male, rather tall, wearing a dark greatcoat, and had a beard. We started across the street but something must have caused him to take alarm. He suddenly abandoned his lurking place, stepped rapidly to the curb, hailed a passing cab, and was gone before we reached the sidewalk. Wanda glanced around for another cab but none were in sight and the opportunity was lost.

"I did manage to get the cab's number," I said. "We may be able to determine where he has gone."

"And I noted the number of the earlier one, also a Red Dragon, so we may be able to determine from whence he had come. Still, I could have played this game better. I should have had you remain in our cab so that you could follow him if he had bolted, or we might simply have gone to the Adler and awaited him there. Now I fear we have simply alerted him to the fact that we know of his existence."

"Should we wait for Baskerville and James?"

"There's no point to it now. They won't be followed again anytime soon. I don't suppose you got a good look at his face?"

"Heavy beard, high forehead. Nothing distinctive enough, particularly if the beard is false. And he might even be using a phantasm mask to change his appearance entirely." I shook my head. "He could even be a slender woman."

"Magical disguises do prove themselves troublesome. But I don't think our shy friend was using anything too elaborate. They're difficult to maintain in dense crowds where you might be jostled and the illusion disturbed. And there are some buildings equipped with unmasking spells that would strip away the disguise instantly. The beard might be false, but if so, it is probably a purely mechanical disguise."

We returned to the office, where Wanda promptly telephoned Albert Fagin, a gangling lad who looks so unlike a detective that he has proven to be quite useful in that capacity. Wanda told him to visit every hotel on the east side of the city and make a request of the concierge or his equivalent in each establishment. "You'll probably have to tip them to get any cooperation, but I'll reimburse you for anything reasonable."

Fagin was to spin a story that he was employed by a man who had paid a visit to the hotel the night before and had somehow misplaced an important piece of paper. Fagin was to request permission to go through the previous day's trash and was to extract every newspaper that was not the Boston Globe. He was then to leaf through any that he found and look for instances where small pieces had been cut out. If he found any such, he was to deliver them to our office, after which he would be paid for his time and trouble.

"Don't lose heart if you find nothing," said Wanda. "I don't think you will, but I would like to confirm my hypothesis."

CHAPTER FIVE

We arrived at the Adler Hotel early, by plan. Wanda had uncovered the identity of a bellhop who was stealing from the guests a year earlier and she had dealt with the matter so judiciously and without adverse publicity that the manager – Morris Severian - was very much in her debt. He appeared promptly at her request and took us back to his private office.

"You might be able to help me slightly with my current client," she explained. "He's one of your guests, Sir Henry Baskerville."

"Oh yes. The Englishman. He's made himself quite popular already. Apparently he tips very well indeed. What would you like to know?"

"In times past, I would have asked to see your register, but everything is electronic or ethereal nowadays. I would like to know who checked in that same evening, but after Sir Henry and his friend, Mr. James."

"That's easy enough." Sebastian uncovered a glowing orb on his desk and made a quick pass with one hand so that it could read his fingerprints. "Only three new guests, I'm afraid. Business has not been brisk this month."

"Could I have the names please?"

"The first was a Joan Watson. I remember her distinctly because I met her in the bar later that evening and she was unusually attractive. Polite, but rather cool. She registered about thirty minutes after your client."

I jotted the name down even though it seemed irrelevant.

"Then there was Arthur Ridgeway. He's a regular, sells high end office equipment I believe. We see him about once a month."

"Could you describe him?"

"Thin, almost fragile looking. Quite short, not much above five feet. Completely bald."

I took more notes, but I was quite sure he was not our man.

"And finally we have Theodore Johnson. I see that he is new to us. I haven't met the man so I can't describe his appearance. He lists Deming, New Mexico, as his home address." He peered at orb more closely. "He requested one of our special rooms for the physically disabled. Mr. Johnson is confined to a wheelchair."

Wanda thanked him for his assistance and we returned to the lobby. "That was more enlightening than it appeared. I think it very unlikely that our mystery man was either Mr. Johnson or Mr. Ridgeway, which means that he did not check into this hotel. That suggests that he might be someone whom Sir Henry would recognize from England and who might have followed him here.."

"Or someone whom Mr. James would know," I suggested.

"An excellent point, Perry. Once again it is negative information, but enough negatives can have a positive outcome. And now let us meet our client once again."

The restaurant in the Adler was both grand and sad. It was grand in the sense that it had been built and furnished in a day when labor was less dear. The walls were covered with inlaid wooden panels, the windows with beveled glass. The curtains were damask, the table linens exquisite, the glassware fine crystal, and the flatware sterling silver. But age had not treated the facilities well. The drapes were limp and stained, the woodwork scratched and pitted, the glassware was no longer as clear as it once had been, and the subdued lighting that had been designed to be romantic was merely dim.

Baskerville and James had already been seated when we arrived. The latter looked mildly bemused but Sir Henry was clearly quite angry. He explained why as soon as we arrived, without even pausing to greet us first.

"They're playing silly games here," he said loudly enough to carry through the room. "I won't be made a fool of."

"What has happened now?" asked Wanda as she took the seat facing Sir Henry.

"One of my shoes has gone missing."

"I thought the prevailing opinion was that it was left behind in customs."

"Not that shoe. Another one. I took my morning's purchases up to the room and notice right away that another was missing. I placed it inside the closet door myself and it was there when I left this morning, but now it's gone. The maid who made up the room insists that she never even looked in the closet, but someone obviously did. I find the whole incident outrageous and insulting, but I imagine you're like Mortimer here and think I'm making an enormous fuss over nothing."

42

"On the contrary, I think this is a very serious development."

"The assistant manager has assured me that they will search the entire hotel, but of course they won't. They'll just pretend to do so to humor me. But I won't be played with."

The waiter appeared with menus and took an order for drinks. Sir Henry and James both ordered wine. Wanda and I opted for coffee.

My meal was a bit overcooked and I noticed that James left a good deal on his plate, but both Wanda and Sir Henry finished what they ordered without apparent complaint. We all had coffee after that and Wanda was the first to address the elephant in the room.

"I tend to agree with your decision to go to Baskerville Manor, Sir Henry. And as quickly as possible. Surrounded by strangers here in the city, you can never be sure who is friend and who is foe. At your estate, you will be able to control to some degree at least who comes and goes and will almost certainly enjoy more privacy if not security."

"We had tentatively agreed to leave directly after this meeting," he said firmly. "I probably should quit myself of this hotel while I still have a complete set of shoes to walk in."

"It is not a short drive but we should be there by evening," ventured James, who was looking very uncomfortable. "I suppose your assessment of the danger is correct, but I confess I still have reservations."

Wanda turned to face him. "Were you aware that you were followed from my office this morning?"

The two men exchanged a puzzled look and both asked the same question almost simultaneously. "Who?"

"We were unable to overtake the man and ascertain his identity. Is there anyone of your acquaintance who wears a full, bushy beard, stands a bit taller than average, and is of moderately heavy build?"

James hesitated for a few seconds, thinking. "Lionel, the butler, has a healthy beard, but I would have described him as somewhat slight of build, though he is taller than most. But what would he be doing in Boston? He and his wife are supposed to be looking after the Manor."

Wanda glanced around and beckoned to the waiter. "Would it be possible to place a call from here?"

"Certainly, madame. I can arrange for a telephone to be brought to you. We no longer keep a clairvoyant on duty."

"A telephone will be just fine."

While we waited, Wanda turned to James. "Were the Lionels named in the will?"

"Yes. They received a generous immediate bequest and provisions were made for their retirement. They have been there for as long as I've known the family, and I believe Lionel's father and mother were similarly employed. His wife comes from the village, a respectable family."

"I assume they knew that they were among the beneficiaries?"

"I know that Charles had told them about the retirement income. I don't know that he ever mentioned the lump sum payment but they would naturally have expected something. It was not enough to make them completely independent, although I suppose they might have managed with whatever other savings they might have. As far as I know, they have no plans to leave their present positions." He glanced at Sir Henry. "Unless they are asked to do so, of course."

"They seem to have been good servants," he commented gruffly. "I certainly wouldn't dispense with them without good reason."

James looked uncomfortable. "I should probably mention that Charles left me some money as well. Not a great deal. Ten thousand dollars. And he had been generous in the past. The small clinic next to my kennel was his idea and he put up most of the money to build it a few years ago. He was a most generous man."

"Were there any other beneficiaries?"

"All of his tenants received a one month forgiveness of their rents. There was a gift to the two town churches, Methodist and Fey, and another to the library. Everything else went to Henry."

"Might I inquire what that amounted to?" Wanda and James both looked to Sir Henry, who looked at first as though he might balk.

"There was close to ten million dollars, plus the Manor and the attached properties. And of course most of the farms in the valley are still legally held in my name, although they are under long term leases and beyond any control I might want to exert for years to come. There's a good income from them, though, and I certainly wouldn't meddle unless it became necessary."

"You are a wealthy man, Sir Henry," Wanda observed. "But I imagine your holdings in England have already proven adequate."

"Barely, I must admit. My parents regained title to the original Baskerville Hall and some of the adjoining properties, but it is not good farming country and much of the land lies unused. The taxes and other expenses have been substantial. I have kept my head above water and have been able to avoid selling back some of what has been recovered for the family, but it has been difficult at times. I won't pretend that this legacy is not going to make my affairs much more manageable in the future."

"Speaking of the future, I gather that you will be the last of the Baskervilles unless you have children of your own."

"I have no living relatives, and my life has been too encumbered to allow me the leisure of pursuing a wife. That too may change now. I trust that I am not too old to enter the contest." There was a hint of genuine enthusiasm in his face, but it passed quickly.

"But if you should die before that happy event occurs, what would then happen to the Baskerville fortune and property? Who would be your heir?"

Sir Henry appeared to be nonplused by the question. "I confess that I have made no will, although I should perhaps repair that situation promptly. In its absence, I assume that it would devolve upon a distant branch of the original family named Peters. Desmond Peters was head of that family the last I knew. He lives in Pennsylvania somewhere and is the pastor of a church. I don't recall the denomination and I have never met the man, although his father and mine corresponded regularly. He has a younger brother but I don't recall his name or indeed anything at all about him."

"It is probably of no consequence." Wanda finished her coffee. "I don't want to delay you much longer as you have a long drive ahead of you, but I do have a proposal."

That proposal had to be postponed because the telephone arrived at that moment. Wanda suggested that Dr. James make the call since he knew the people involved and he did so, engaged in a brief conversation making use of a flimsy excuse. He hung up and looked solemn.

"I spoke to Mrs. Lionel. She said that her husband was in the village running some errands and was not expected back until late in the afternoon. So he might be back in Vermont, or he might not be."

Wanda's face betrayed nothing of her thoughts. "Well, then, I propose that you, Sir Henry, avail yourself of a companion, a reliable man who does not have the demeanor of a bodyguard, but who will be alert to any danger that might arise and prove to be a safe confidant. I cannot at present leave Boston because of two pending cases although I hope to join you at the earliest possible moment."

Baskerville appeared uncertain. "I appreciate your concern and it's certainly not a bad idea, but where could I find someone with those attributes and immediate availability on such short notice?"

Wanda turned to look at me. "My assistant, Mr. Everdeen, should fill the bill nicely. I assure you that he has all the qualities you could wish for. And as it happens, your route north passes quite close to his home so it would only require a short delay for him to pack a bag."

Needless to say, the offer took me completely by surprise, but I did my best to look as though I had expected it.

"I will do my best for you, Sir Henry."

CHAPTER SIX

One rather peculiar event occurred as we were preparing to leave the hotel. The desk clerk hailed us as we were passing by and said that a telephone message had been left for us. Lionel, the butler, had called from Baskerville Manor to ask whether Mr. James or Sir Henry had wanted anything urgent and apologized for being away when the original call was made. Wanda didn't say anything but I had a mental reservation. We still didn't know for certain that it was Lionel himself who had called, or for that matter from whence the call had originated. He could just as easily be in Boston and, having been alerted to our interest by his wife, have pretended to be calling from Vermont.

The peculiar event was that the clerk also said that Sir Henry's missing shoe had been found. He fumbled around behind the desk and produced the object in question. "We found it in a trash bin near the rear exit. I can't imagine how it ended up there. Is this your missing shoe, Sir Henry?"

"Yes it is." He accepted the shoe and regarded it with a puzzled expression. Wanda was about to leave when he asked her to wait a second. "This is quite strange. It's my missing shoe, all right, but it's not the one that went missing here. This is the one that we had supposed fell prey to the carelessness of your customs department."

"Then they must both have gone missing since we arrived at the hotel," said Dr. James. "How mystifying."

"Yes, isn't it?" commented Wanda and then she left with promises to join us as soon as possible in Vermont.

Wanda returned to the office where, later that day, she had a visit from Fagin, the substance of which I was not to learn until much later. He had completed his sweep of all of the hotels she had indicated and had found a dozen or so newspapers other than Globe, but none of them showed any evidence of having been clipped. She had expected this, however, and was not particularly disappointed.

I must vary a bit further from a straightforward narrative of my involvement here. While I was traveling homeward in James' aging but roomy Studebaker, Wanda set out to visit the dispatcher's office for the Red Dragon taxicab company.

She had more luck than usual. Not only was the dispatcher able to identify the two operators who had served our mystery man, but the one who followed our clients when they left our office was on the premises at the time while the other who had unwittingly aided his escape was due to turn in his cab and go off shift within the hour.

Wanda described the first man as a surly type whose natural inclination was to lie in preference to the truth, even when it availed him nothing, but she had cultivated the dispatcher's friendship in the past and he told the man curtly to answer to the best of his knowledge. His name was Claymore Johnson and he admitted that he'd picked up a fare that morning who requested that he follow a party from the Adler Hotel, then hover near our address so that the front entrance was visible. He had subsequently agreed to follow the cab pointed out to him.

"The man said that he was a detective and there was nothing against the law about following another party. He promised me a healthy tip and I saw no reason to refuse it."

"Of course not," admitted Wanda. "Can you describe him?"

"Biggish sort, all wrapped up in a heavy greatcoat. He had a thick beard what needed trimming. And he had dark eyebrows that almost met."

"What was his voice like?"

"Deep, but a little hoarse. Like he'd had a cold. He didn't say much."

"Would you recognize him if you saw him again?"

Johnson became wary. "Might. Never saw him directly though. Just through the mirror. He was sitting behind me, wasn't he?"

"Is there anything else you can tell me about him?"

"Sure. I can tell you his name. He told it to me while he was paying me off."

"And what was his name then?"

"He called himself Charles Baskervelt, or Baskerton, or something like that."

"Could it have been Baskerville?"

"Could have been. I didn't take particular note of it."

"Just where did you pick up Mr. Baskerville?"

"Down on the common. He was my first fare this morning, right after seven. Flagged me down and told me he was investigating a pair of jewel thieves. Offered a bonus if I was helpful."

Johnson had been discharged and paid as promised when his passenger disembarked across the street from the sporting goods store. There had been no place to park and he would have been too conspicuous hanging about. Wanda thanked him for his information, passed him a ten dollar bill, and waited patiently for the other man to arrive.

He was a bit early, which was all to the good. He was also much more forthcoming, although nothing he said added substantially to what Wanda already knew. Our quarry had flagged him down, presumably having caught sight of us crossing to where he stood, and had told the driver – Roger Ackroyd – that he was late for his flight out of Logan Airport.

"He seemed upset when he first got in, but he settled down after that and didn't say anything even when we got stuck in slow traffic at the tunnel."

The ride ended at the departure lane, but Ackroyd had noticed something odd. "I got held up behind a bus when I pulled out and I happened to look into the rearview mirror. He never went inside the airport. I saw him walking toward the taxi ranks and then I lost him when one of the shuttles pulled in. It struck me as a bit odd at the time, but it was none of my business."

Ackroyd's description added nothing to what Wanda already knew. She parted with another ten dollars, thanked the dispatcher, and returned to the office.

By that point, I had already loaded a hastily packed bag into the Studebaker's back seat – the trunk was already filled with Sir Henry's luggage. He had rather a lot, but then again, I gathered from his conversation with Mr. James that he planned on an extended stay. He had added a brand new shotgun and a pair of pistols, each of which was still boxed, along with ammunition. He had assured us that his property in England was being ably administered by a management firm and he felt he could safely ignore it until "the present mysteries are resolved." Concealed in my own bag was a handgun, a mechanical one, which I had never had occasion to use outside a firing range.

James drove the entire distance, politely declining my offer to spell him behind the wheel. He insisted that he was a terrible passenger and would be far more at ease as he was. There was some desultory conversation between the two at first – details about the Manor, the tenant farms, and the trust that governed most of the estate's investments – but they were very boring and I only listened out of a sense of duty. It was clear that Dr. James had only a superficial understanding of the financial side of Charles Baskerville.

I had worked for Wanda long enough to know that much of the work in an investigation is routine and boring, but this was almost as dry as poring through old records searching for births, deaths, and marriages. They lapsed into silence after an hour or so, and I was frankly just as happy that they did so. I could then entertain my own thoughts and I enthusiastically began reviewing everything that had happened, everything that we had learned since James first showed up at our office door. I might only be a temporary assistant detective, but I was determined to live up to my ephemeral title.

Wanda had told me to call her every day, more often if I learned anything that seemed significant. "Keep me advised of anything unusual that you may see, hear, or learn of, even if it seems irrelevant. And keep your wits about you. There is danger at Baskerville Manor, natural or supernatural. It has taken one life already and could just as readily take another."

She was particularly interested in interactions between Sir Henry and his neighbors and tenants. "And don't forget the servants. The Lionels are not above suspicion. Take nothing for granted and stay alert. I suggest you take detailed notes because there might be periods of time in which I am unavailable. Don't rely on your memory."

We had come up with a cover story to explain my presence to the community. I was a temporary secretary – all of my job descriptions seemed to contain that qualifier – whom Sir Henry had engaged in Boston to help him with the early stages of his assumption of the handling of his inheritance. I would use my own name and actually would be acting in my assumed capacity. James had assured us that Charles Baskerville's affairs were above board and profitable, but extremely complex. "He used to devote at least one full day a week just to correspondence and a review of invoices and payments. I suggested more than once that he hire someone to oversee the household accounts, but he thought that the Lionels might take offense and continued to monitor them himself."

The drive was quite scenic. Spring had advanced to the point where there were flowers in bloom and the branches of trees were cloaked with leaves, but we seemed to travel slowly back in time as we proceeded north. There were even a few bare trees – although the fuzziness of fresh buds was evident – and we encountered unrepaired frost heaves in the roadway. The towns through which we passed grew generally smaller and more picturesque and the trees were taller, broader, and grew more densely.

Drear Valley, Vermont, site of Baskerville Manor, was almost an hour north of Stowe, the last good sized community through which we passed. Dusk had fallen by then and I was restless. We had stopped to eat at a seafood restaurant south of Montpelier, but had otherwise been sitting for seven hours. I confess that I was dozing off, my analysis of the case long since having ended with no particular insights, when Dr. James announced that we were nearing our destination. It was the first words any of us had spoken for at least an hour.

We had been driving uphill for some time at that point and there appeared to be an unbroken wall of worn down mountains barring our path. There were no streetlights here and I was a city dweller; the darkness seemed to have a deeper quality than any I had previously experienced. The road suddenly jogged to the right and there was a narrow gap, barely visible, which led over the crest of a hill. Drear Valley unfurled itself below us.

The road ahead dropped suddenly and acutely and it seemed only a matter of seconds before we were traveling through a landscape of gnarled trees, sluggish bogs, and occasional rocky prominences. Although we had seen the lights of civilization from the crest, they were completely invisible to us for the next fifteen or twenty minutes. The end of the wasteland was also quite abrupt. We broke out of the trees and saw lights stretching away in every direction except to our rear.

"The village is about four miles ahead, but the turn for Baskerville Manor is shortly before that. I assume that you prefer to go directly there, Henry."

"I admit that I'm anxious to see the property, although I imagine most of my inspection will have to wait until daylight."

"I believe you'll find it quite welcoming. Charles – your uncle – took great pride in his home and spared no expense to maintain it. It was the only area in which he spent relatively freely."

"Family pride is a strong characteristic among the Baskervilles," said Sir Henry. "I believe you will see little has changed in that regard."

I was fairly confident that we had not been followed. There had been little traffic for the last two hours and in fact I hadn't noticed a single vehicle moving in either direction for almost half of that time. Unless someone was operating with the headlights off – which was entirely possible if they were equipped with an infrared charm of some sort – we had been alone for some time. Of course, there was no secret about where we were bound so it would have been completely unnecessary to shadow us. The mysterious stranger might well be ahead of us awaiting our arrival.

"Where does the name come from?" I asked. "Drear Valley, I mean. It doesn't sound very welcoming."

"It was originally settled by John and Anthony Drear, brothers, just before the Revolution. They owned the entire valley and built the original house where the Manor now stands. Nothing of it remains now except the old stable and some of the stone walls. When the Baskervilles emigrated from England, they planned to create their own demesne, a kind of self contained world where they could simulate the England that they felt no longer existed elsewhere. Their attitude changed over the course of generations, of course, but even though Charles was quite enlightened in some ways, he reveled in being the lord of the Manor."

"It's in our blood," added Sir Henry. "There are certain bloodlines which are foreordained to rise above the hoi polloi. But at the same time, we recognize our obligations to those dependent upon us. It is not such a privileged position as one might suppose."

"And I imagine it does help to have lots of money." This was greeted with what I thought was a touch of stiffness and I realized I had been tactless, although in fairness it was in response to muted snobbery. Rather than compound the error, I lapsed into a more discreet silence for the rest of the trip.

The outer gate was open, as expected, and so was the inner, presumably at the direction of the Lionels, who knew that we were to arrive that evening. James drove directly to the front door, which was flanked by Corinthian columns that appeared to be genuine granite. There were two figures standing at the door and I realized they must have seen the lights of the Studebaker when we turned off the main road. There was a short stretch of open land there before we would have been once again concealed by the trees.

I assumed that I was about to meet the Lionels.

CHAPTER EIGHT

It was indeed the Lionels who descended the steps to greet us, followed by a younger man – not much more than a boy – whom I had not noticed. I was particularly interested in Barry Lionel's physical appearance. His build approximated that of the man who had followed Sir Henry in Boston and he certainly had a full beard. I was of two minds about identifying him, nevertheless, because there seemed something in his posture that was unfamiliar, and I thought the man I had seen jump into the cab had been broader in the shoulders. I could not really be certain either way. I would have guessed his age as late fifties, but hair and beard were still quite dark and he might have been younger.

His wife, Beatrice, I judged to be his contemporary. She was shorter than he and perhaps a bit on the heavy side, though not excessively. I am tempted to describe her features as plain, but that was only true when she was in repose. Her smile was quite attractive and lent an entirely different tone to her face. Like her husband, she seemed sturdy and reliable.

The third figure was introduced as Billy, a village boy who sometimes helped out with odd jobs. He said not a word, just nodded, and was put to work unloading the luggage and carrying it inside. Sir Henry had turned to look back over the valley, but much of it was concealed by the descending ranks of trees that separated the Manor from the road.

Dr. James must have read his thoughts because he leaned toward him and touched his arm. "The view is much better from the library. You can see fully two thirds of the valley from there."

"Where was my uncle found? His body, I mean."

Lionel pointed to a murky patch of darkness. "You can't really see it from here, but it was around behind that small copse of trees. I can take you there in the morning if you wish."

"We'll see. Let's go inside, shall we? It's a bit nippy."

It was cooler than I was used to so I was happy when we all moved inside. The front hall was nearly the size of the apartment I shared with Julia, and for the first time I began to get a sense of how very different were the lives of the wealthy. A wide staircase led to the upper floors and there were doors to our left and right, and another beyond the staircase.

Sir Henry was either restless from our long confinement during the drive or genuinely curious about the Manor because he immediately requested a full tour. Mrs. Lionel announced that she would set out a light meal in the dining room while we were so engaged, not having prepared anything more substantial because of her uncertainty about the time of our arrival. Sir Henry thanked her and assured her that whatever she could manage would be fine with him.

We paused only long enough for Lionel to instruct Billy to lock the doors when he was done. "A prisoner escaped from the Sebastian prison yesterday morning. The authorities believe that he has headed north toward the Canadian border, but we have all been warned to take precautions, just in case he has remained in the vicinity after all. The man is considered to be quite dangerous. He was serving a life sentence for murder."

"Who was it?" asked James. "I donate some of my time at the prison clinic and know most of the inmates. It wasn't Selden, by any chance? He's tried twice to escape."

"Yes, sir. It was indeed Richard Selden. They say he killed his best friend, although there's always been some doubt about the witness whose testimony convicted him."

James shook his head. "It was a brutal crime if I remember it correctly. Selden insisted that it was self defense but his victim was reportedly a gentle man and not nearly a physical match for his killer. I can't imagine how they could be so careless as to let him loose. More budget cuts, no doubt. Our parsimonious state legislature will save us into ruin if they keep at it."

Lionel looked as though he might have more to say, but apparently he thought better of it.

"Is all secure here?" Sir Henry turned his head to indicate he meant the Manor at large.

"I believe so, sir. We have modern locks on all the doors and windows, and I check everything before I retire for the night. I have a complete set of keys for you, of course. Unfortunately we are unable to make use of necromantic wards." He turned to look at Dr. James. "I assume you have told Sir Henry about our peculiar circumstances with regard to magical devices."

James nodded. "Sir Henry may, of course, choose to alter that situation."

Baskerville cleared his throat. "It's too soon to think about that just now. We will have to rely on mechanical protections. I don't suppose there are dogs?"

"No, sir," said Lionel. "Not any longer. The Master, your uncle that is, closed the kennels when he inherited the estate. He was never one for hunting. We used to keep a collie after that, but she died a few years ago and we never had the heart to replace her."

We were about to start on our tour when James hesitated. "If you can spare me, Henry, I think I'll head home. My wife will be expecting me and I am frankly rather tired."

"You will miss the repast Mrs. Lionel has prepared for us."

"Sadly, yes. Her concoctions are second in quality only to those of my Abigail. I must rise early tomorrow as well to see about some of my patients and my prize bitch should be ready to drop a litter. But I will be available later in the day if there is anything that you need from me."

I confess that I felt a faint sense of abandonment when the man left. Sir Henry had treated me respectfully enough, but there was a distance between us that I didn't properly recognize until I realized that the same separation was manifest between himself and Lionel. I was a servant, not a companion. I doubt that Sir Henry himself was aware of his own class distinctions, which I imagine were common among the English aristocracy, but he had a habit of looking at my forehead rather than into my eyes. I wasn't sure whether to be amused or offended.

The tour was briskly done but comprehensive. The ground floor consisted of a large dining room where Mrs. Lionel was bustling about, a morning room furnished with small tables and comfortable chairs, the kitchen proper into which we looked only in passing, a small but modern bathroom that was obviously a recent addition, a sitting room with a large fire place, a music room that contained only a piano covered with a dusty sheet, a small den, and the servants' quarters, most of which were closed up. Only the Lionels lived in the Manor though occasionally temporary help would spend a night or two as guests.

There were six bedrooms and two baths upstairs, not counting the private bath that Sir Henry would use. The master bedroom was quite grand although Sir Henry did not appear to care for the manner in which it had been furnished. The other five bedrooms – one of which contained my bag – were all in good order although Lionel informed us that there had been few guests in recent years. "The wife has taken off the sheets and pillow cases and put them away until they are needed. There should be fresh towels as well."

Fully one third of this floor was given over to the library, which was fully stocked and, judging by the condition of those few books which I examined, heavily used. "Mr. Charles devoted several hours each day to reading," said Lionel. "He would usually sit at the window as he did so." It was a large bay window and from that vantage point we could indeed see the greater part of the valley spread below. I noticed a denser cluster of lights and Lionel confirmed that this was the village.

Sir Henry showed an almost boyish enthusiasm and pronounced himself well satisfied with what he had seen. "My uncle generally had good taste, I am happy to say. I will be making few changes around here, you may rest assured, Lionel."

The butler appeared to be mildly uncomfortable. "We served your uncle for many years and were happy to do so. He was a gentleman of an age that has largely passed, an age to which my wife and I also belong. It seems to us that you would likely be happier with servants more in tune with the times."

"I have heard nothing that inclines me to dispense with your services, Lionel. You may reassure your wife that her position – and yours naturally – are perfectly secure."

Lionel looked even more ill at ease. "I thank you for your confidence, sir, but perhaps it would be for the best if stayed only long enough for you to get the feel of the place and make your own arrangements."

"Do I understand that you are giving notice?"

"Not in so many words, sir. We intend to stay on for as long as you feel necessary. But Mr. Charles' death was quite a shock to us both and we no longer feel that this is our home. We have saved diligently through the years and your uncle was most generous when he was alive and in his subsequent remembrance of us. My wife's sister in Providence died recently and left us her house and we can live quite comfortably in retirement. We are both looking forward to a life of less responsibility."

Sir Henry looked distinctly uncomfortable, but he was gracious about it. "Well, I confess to feeling slightly as though I were to be abandoned, but I can understand your point of view. And while I am happy enough with the arrangements as they are, there inevitably will be changes and I imagine that the contrast might be painful for the two of you. Let us leave it that we will consider the matter again once I have properly settled in and that we will reach a mutual understanding so that we part on friendly terms. I owe it to my uncle, if not common human decency, to see that neither of you suffers unnecessarily from his death."

"Thank you, sir." Lionel looked distinctly relieved as he led us back to the dining room, where a sumptuous meal awaited us. I discovered that I was ravenous and set to with enthusiasm. There was cold meat and cheese and smoked fish and a hearty salad. Lionel served drinks. I settled for a dark German beer but Sir Henry preferred brandy.

We ate in relative silence and put scarcely a dent into the food, but Lionel assured us it would not be wasted. "The grounds are in need of a spring clean up and other maintenance. I have taken the liberty or engaging a crew to perform the work over the next few days. I would have preferred to have it done before you arrived, sir, but competent help is in short supply and long demand."

Sir Henry waved it off. "If I've learned anything in life, it's that railing against the inevitable is a waste of time. Is there a motorcar, by the way? Or did my uncle walk everywhere?"

"There are two automobiles in the garage, formerly the stable. One is a late model sedan. The other is more of a touring car. Your uncle always drove himself, however, so we employ no chauffeur. Oh, and there is a small and rather disreputable truck but I'm not sure if it still runs. It hasn't been used in years."

"I've driven myself before, although it's not my favorite pastime. And I'll have to adjust to your American insistence upon using the wrong side of the road." He glanced in my direction. "Do you drive, Mr. Everdeen?"

I assured him that I did, although I did not own a car of my own. "It's more hindrance than help in a large city."

"Then perhaps I can ask you to do the honors tomorrow. I would like to familiarize myself with the lay of the land and the village in particular."

"I'm at your service."

We finished our meal and a second drink each, then decided to retire for the evening as it was getting on toward midnight. I considered calling Wanda to advise her of our safe arrival, but it was late enough that she might well have gone to her own bed and I decided that my first report could wait until the morning.

Sir Henry and I walked upstairs together and when we reached the top landing, he spoke softly, perhaps the first time he had actually addressed me as an equal. "I wouldn't say this in front of Lionel, but I confess I find the atmosphere here somewhat oppressive. It's probably just the after effects of the long drive and knowing that my uncle died here under mysterious circumstances, but I will certainly lock my bedroom door tonight and I suggest that you do the same."

"You don't suspect the Lionels?"

He shook his head. "No, of course not. They seem a bit dour but not at all unreliable, and they were with my uncle for decades. I would feel more comfortable if we could employ an Astral Barrier or an Aura of Confusion, but locks and chains should serve us well enough."

We bid each other good night and went to our respective rooms.

I was in one of the smaller bedrooms, which was only three times the size of the one Julia and I shared. The sheets were fresh – I assume that Mrs. Lionel had made up the bed that very day – and some clean towels had been laid out on a table near the door. I was directly across the hall from one of the bathrooms.

It only took a few minutes to unpack and my small selection of clothing was lost in the immense armoire that stood in one corner. I never even opened the drawers in the two matching chests that flanked it. There was a single window in the room and I stood at it briefly, staring down at a lighter space in the darkness which I eventually realized was the private cemetery that stood to one side of the Manor house. I fancied that I saw movement there and stared for quite some time, but if so, there was no recurrence and it might easily have been the shadow of a cloud cast by the nearly full moon. It was a clear night and the stars seemed uncommonly bright, but then again, I had rarely spent a night outside the city with its smog and halo of lights.

The house seemed almost preternaturally quiet, and this too was the difference between city and country. There were no traffic noises, no ambulances sirens, no aircraft making a late landing at the airport. I undressed and got into bed, vaguely uneasy, but dismissed it as an understandable reaction to a strange environment.

It was a stranger environment than I realized.

CHAPTER NINE

We ate breakfast in the morning room which took advantage of the sunlight that advanced upon us through a natural gap in the mountains. Sir Henry was cheerful but preoccupied and set about his food with considerable enthusiasm. Mrs. Lionel served us efficiently and politely, but with no particular warmth. I had the distinct impression that she was deeply troubled about something. Although I had slept only reasonably well – not uncommon when I was in a strange place –the hot food and brilliant sunlight had improved my mood immeasurably.

I had dreamed during the night, or so I assumed. I had a distinct memory of the sound of a weeping woman, and thought that I had risen from my bed and walked to the door of my room, only to have the sound cease before I reached it. I may actually have done so, but now it seemed to me that the weeping had been imaginary. There was no woman in the house, after all, except Mrs. Lionel, whose quarters were likely too far away for me to have heard her unless she had shouted at the top of her lungs. When I mentioned this to Sir Henry in passing, he stiffened slightly and then said that he'd had a similar experience.

"I too thought it was no more than a dream, but a common experience suggests otherwise."

"It may have been some other sound that we misinterpreted. A peculiarity of the wind, perhaps, or some nocturnal bird."

"Let's ask Mrs. Lionel." And when she returned to bring us fresh coffee, we did that very thing.

She appeared somewhat disturbed by the question but quickly recovered. "There's no woman here except myself, sir, and I assure you that my sleep was peaceful last night. There's a young girl who comes in most days to help in the kitchen, but she never spends the night unless the weather is bad."

Sir Henry thanked her and seemed to take her at her word. I was not as readily convinced. I had the distinct feeling that she had just told us a lie, although I had no way of determining the truth. Her husband appeared a moment later to tell us that the smaller automobile had been brought to the front of the Manor in anticipation of our using it. I once again considered the possibility that he was our mystery man from London but was still unable to form an opinion. In many ways he was a physical match, but some of the details varied enough to leave doubt. Of course, I had seen the unknown shadower only in fits and starts and from a distance. And what possible motive could he have had for spying on his new employer, particularly given his decision to resign his position in the near future?

Despite his avowed interest in a grand tour, Sir Henry decided to defer the trip until later in the day. "Just before we checked out of the hotel, I received a telegram from my manager back in London and there is some paperwork I need to deal with." It sounded more like an excuse than an explanation, but I was in no position to question him.

I stepped outside intending to stroll through the garden, but there were at least six workmen there and a pair of trucks bulging with shears, rakes, shovels, saws, and other implements of destruction. This was undoubtedly the work crew Lionel had mentioned the night before, and I didn't want to get in their way. Thwarted from my original intention, I walked along the driveway, trying to guess just where Charles Baskerville had met his death. There was nothing to mark the spot, of course, and any physical remnants of that night's activities had long since been erased by the spring thaw and fresh grass.

I had just reached the end of the low wall when I saw a young man walking steadily toward me from the direction of the main road. He nodded a greeting once he was close enough and I wished him a good morning.

"Are you here for the gardens?" I asked. "The others are already hard at work."

"No, sir. Mr. Lionel hired me to do some painting."

It occurred to me that I might find out something useful if I asked the right questions. "When was that?"

"Day before yesterday. I've done some odd jobs for him in the past and he knows I'll do a good job." He sounded mildly defensive.

"I'm sure you do. Mr. Lionel doesn't strike me as the kind to be taken advantage of. Did he speak to you directly?"

He shrugged. "Yes and no. He stopped by my house a week past and told me that there was some work available if I wanted it, but I was engaged by Miss Staples to build as fence around her garden and I told him I couldn't get to it until this week. He said there was no hurry and that he would be in touch and then two days ago Mrs. Lionel calls on the telephone and tells me that her husband wanted to know if I was still interested and I said yes."

"So you didn't actually speak to him at the time."

He was clearly puzzled by the question, but answered promptly. "Not that time, no, I didn't. But Mrs. Lionel has engaged me in the past as well. Is there something wrong?"

"Not at all. I've just arrived and I wondered how this kind of arrangement was made."

"Are you the new one, then? Mr. Baskerville?"

"No, I'm just his secretary. Sir Henry is inside."

"What's he like then? Everyone will be asking me about him."

I decided that I wasn't acting like a discreet private secretary. "I've only just started to work for him myself so I really can't say. He seems fair minded enough."

"There are some who are worried. Mr. Charles was well liked. He did a lot of good things for the people around here."

"I'm sure everything will work out." I stepped back. "I shouldn't keep you from your work."

He nodded again and headed up toward the house.

I walked about a bit more, trying to look at things the way Wanda might, but that recalled to me the fact that I had yet to report back to her, so I returned to the house. Lionel showed me to the sitting room where a phone sat by a comfortable chair and I called the office. Wanda picked it up on the second ring.

I believe that I provided her with a succinct but comprehensive summary of everything that had happened since we'd left Boston. I considered leaving out the mysterious crying in the night but decided to include it in my narration. Wanda asked a couple of questions to which I supplied answers.

"You're doing fine, Perry. Keep your eyes and ears open and remember that anything might prove relevant, however unlikely. I'm afraid you're going to be on your own for a few days. I picked up another client this morning and the job is going to take me away from the city. It's imperative that I act quickly. In fact, I'm not certain where exactly I'm going to be so you won't be able to get in touch with me. I'll try to call you from time to time, but it might be difficult. I'll explain it all when I can. But don't worry if you don't hear from me for as much as a week."

I felt an odd sense of abandonment, mixed with pride that Wanda trusted me to continue this particular investigation on my own. Once our conversation was done, I called Julia and told her that I was working on a case and wouldn't be home for a few days, then gave her the number for the Manor.

"Nothing dangerous, is it?"

I assured her – although I had no basis for the opinion – that I was as safe as houses. "I'm just doing some secretarial work for a client, a genuine English lord, no less. And I'm staying in a mansion with a butler and a cook."

"Don't get used to the easy life," she cautioned. "I'll cook for you but you do your own butlering."

Sir Henry reappeared shortly after ten and a few minutes later I was rather cautiously driving the two of us down the gravel drive. I had to pause to open the smaller gate, which Lionel had apparently closed following our arrival, but we reached the main road with no difficulty and turned right toward the village.

Grimalkin was even smaller than I had imagined, a cluster of buildings grouped around the intersection of the main road and a shorter and narrower one that only extended a few blocks in either direction. There were a few businesses – a diner, a small independent grocer, a drug store, two bars, and a larger store that specialized in farm supplies and dispensed gasoline. The schoolhouse was tiny – there was no high school so presumably children that age were bussed outside the valley – and the library was even smaller. The two churches stood at opposite ends, about as far from each other as it was possible to get. The healing clinic was almost hidden from view by pine trees but a sign that read "Mortimer James, HD" identified it for us. Behind the clinic and attached to it was a larger house and beyond that a series of caged enclosures which I assumed were the kennels. I wondered what kind of noise suppressing spells he used to keep the dogs from irritating his neighbors with their barking.

There were perhaps a dozen private homes in the immediate area, one of which advertised rooms to let. I estimated as many as twice that at the opposite end of the village. There were very few

people about but those we did pass glanced at us with frank
curiosity.

Sir Henry declined to stop. "I just want a general overview at this
point. I'll meet people later." So I followed the road north out of
town. It ran almost perfectly straight until we neared the far end of
the valley where it began to twist and turn because of the rougher
terrain, which resembled that through which we had passed upon
entering the valley the previous evening, although this piece of
wilderness was much smaller.

I found a place to turn around – it was more difficult than it
seemed because the road had become quite narrow, and we returned.
I suggested that we try one or more of the dirt roads, which provided
access to the individual farms, but Sir Henry seemed to have tired of
his tour already.

"Perhaps tomorrow. I've spent enough time sitting in
automobiles to last me for a while and frankly I'm in the mood for
lunch."

So we returned to Baskerville Manor where Lionel met us and
said that he'd see to the car while we went inside. "Mrs. Lionel has
prepared a hearty soup and a light casserole."

The food was excellent. I thought Baskerville would be losing a
gem if the Lionels did in fact retire. I could never mention this to
Julia, however, who was quite proud of her skill in the kitchen. She
could have learned a great deal from Mrs. Lionel though.

After we'd eaten, Sir Henry announced that he planned to spend
the afternoon sitting in his library. "I need to settle in properly for a
bit." He summoned Lionel and asked him to send some brandy and
a glass. Then he turned to me. "We'll start on the paperwork
tomorrow, I think, so I won't need your service any further today. I
imagine you can find something to entertain yourself."

An idea immediately occurred to me. "Actually, if I might use
the car, I'd like to go into the village for a while. There are a few
things I forgot to pack in the rush and I imagine I can find what I
need. I might be an hour or two."

"Take as long as you like."

Lionel insisted that I take a key with me so I followed him to his
pantry where a key box was affixed to one wall. There were several
rows of keys, all neatly labeled. "Mr. Charles replaced most of the

locks but he failed to do so in an organized fashion. It was most unlike him. This one is for the front door."

Lionel told me that the car was still where I'd left it so I asked if there was anything I might pick up for the house while I was there. He thanked me for my consideration but assured me that he and his wife were amply supplied.

This time I had a definite destination in mind and within a few minutes I was parking in front of the clinic. I intended to pay a brief visit to Dr. James to ask him if he had any explanation for the announcement by the Lionels that they planned to leave Baskerville Manor. Almost as soon as I was out of the car, however, I was being hailed by a stranger, a man somewhat older than myself, who emerged from the private house that faced the clinic from across the street. He was a tall man and quite solidly built, clean shaven and with short hair. His skin was dark enough that I assumed there was African blood in his background.

"You must be the secretary," he said while enthusiastically pumping mys hand. "Mortimer mentioned you last night. I'm Dennis Staples. Pleased to meet you."

The name was vaguely familiar and I remembered that Dr. James had mentioned that there was a botanist staying in the village. He was studying some unusual fungus or toadstool that flourished in the valley and had rented a room because the project was expected to consume the best part of a year.

I gave him my name and explained that I was acting as secretary to Sir Henry.

"How is the new man settling in?"

I gave a politic answer to the effect that it was quite early days yet but that he seemed to be pleased with the Manor.

"Then he'll be staying here permanently, do you think? The locals are rather in a dither about it. They're afraid that he'll return to England and break up the estate for sale. That would mean a new landlord with all the attendant uncertainties, to say nothing of the fact that Charles Baskerville was a generous man who supported the community in many less than obvious ways."

"I would say that his present intention is to remain for at least some time to come. The family seat is, however, in England and I couldn't begin to guess what might happen in the long run."

Staples looked briefly uncomfortable. "Is he a superstitious man, do you think?"

"I'd say not."

"He's not apprehensive about the so-called family curse then?"

"He scoffs at it actually. Which is not to say that he isn't taking precautions. But he feels that some human agency must be involved, despite what the authorities may have concluded."

"I am a man of science. I know that the hippogriff is almost certainly a creature of mythology. But I also know that magical beings do exist. It's entirely possible that some perfectly natural beast might be mistaken for one. You're familiar with the circumstances of Charles' death?"

I admitted that I was.

"Then isn't it entirely possible that a griffin or perhaps a harpy attacked him, for whatever reason?"

"And the hoof prints?"

"Unrelated. Some perfectly mundane animal may have passed at some point and left its mark."

"And how would a griffin have penetrated the warding spell that protects the manor? Baskerville was well inside when he was attacked."

"Griffins are natural creatures. They would not be bothered by a barrier meant to reject the arcane."

He was right and I should have realized that. "Do you think that Sir Henry is in danger?"

Staples shook his head. "I have no opinion on the matter. It is my understanding that the family curse was nullified some generations back. In any case, I can't imagine why the curse would have fallen on Charles Baskerville, who was probably the most decent man I have ever met. I believe that there is a mystery here and that it hasn't played itself out yet. I suggest you keep your wits about you while you are here."

"I try to do that wherever I might be."

"Well, please keep in mind then that if you ever desire an ally or confidant, I am at your service."

I was suspicious of his motives and it must have shown in my face, because he responded with animation. "Please don't think that I'm just a busybody. The nature of my profession is to seek the answers to mysteries, and I feel that there is something very mysterious indeed regarding Charles Baskerville's death. I would be a poor scientist if I wasn't curious. But I don't mean to suggest anything inappropriate. Your loyalty to your employer must come first."

The day had grown unusually warm and I found that I was perspiring freely. Staples must have noticed as well because he changed tack directly. "Hot, isn't it? Might I offer you some lemonade? My cousin keeps a cold pitcher of it in the refrigerator." He gestured back toward the house from which he'd come.

"You live with your cousin, then?"

"Indeed I do. My housing stipend for this project would not suffice for anything fancier, if anything fancier even existed in the valley. I'm working on a grant to study the life cycle of a rather innocuous looking plant that somehow generates the kind of aura one normally associates with animals. My cousin charges me a nominal fee and I lend a hand when it's needed."

"Now that you mention it, I believe Dr. James mentioned that you were conducting some sort of long term study."

"About which I promise to tell you nothing further unless solicited to do so. Even I find it rather dull at times, but once started, it must be finished, or I would face some rather stiff questions from my financial backers. In any case I'm enjoying a brief respite today. I've trudged through the swamps and climbed over uncaring rocks and stumbled through tenacious vines already this morning and my duty is done until tomorrow when I have to retrace my steps and take more measurements and so forth."

"Aren't you a bit concerned that you'll run into the escaped convict? Aren't there rumors that he's hiding out somewhere in the valley?"

"Any man clever enough to escape from prison would certainly be smart enough to avoid our local wilderness. There is a reason the local farmers have made no effort to clear the land at either end of the valley. It's almost as if the landscape was consciously resisting the encroachments of civilization. But come along. I'm thirsty myself."

I was about to decline because I had come there expressly to speak to Dr. James, but then I remembered that Wanda had suggested that I try to learn what the local people thought about the death of Charles Baskerville. This seemed too good an opportunity to be lost, so I thanked him and admitted that a cool drink would suit me well.

And so I found myself seated at a table in a pleasantly laid out kitchen. The cousin was introduced as Dolores Staples, who must have been about thirty years of age and who was a shade darker even than her cousin. She was friendly enough, although she left us alone at the earliest possible moment, explaining that it was her day to do the laundry.

"Dolores is so organized that she puts me to shame," said Staples. "Woe to anyone who disrupts her schedule without sufficient reason."

"Did you know Charles Baskerville?" I asked, trying to make the question sound casual.

"Certainly. I doubt you'll find anyone in the valley who didn't. Terrible thing, his death. The entire community was in mourning."

"I've not heard the whole story but I gather the circumstances were peculiar."

He gave a short, humorless laugh. "That's an understatement. The man died of fright, or at least that's what everyone believes. The medical examiner won't say anything beyond heart failure or a stroke, despite the wounds on his face."

"He was attacked then?"

"It seems so, though no one can venture a rational explanation that isn't too farfetched. You've heard of the family curse?"

"I know that there was one at some time, but wasn't it brought to an end long ago?"

"There are varying opinions about that. Personally I believe that there is a kind of cosmic karma, if you will, that transcends both science and the arcane. The Baskerville family has never been a lucky one, and that trait has affected both the good and the bad among them."

"It's supposed to involve a hippogriff, isn't it?"

Staples nodded. "That's the story. But hippogriffs don't exist. They can't even be cobbled together necromantically. The DNA is too disparate. But it could easily be that both a horse and a griffin were involved back in England, separately, and the same could well be true here."

"You think then that the curse could manifest itself in two separate bodies and cause them to work in consort?"

"That would be one solution, but it wouldn't explain the death of Charles Baskerville. His property is warded against all forms of magic. You may have noticed that none of your personal charms will work inside the house."

Obviously I'd known that in advance, but I nodded as though having just realized the truth of what he was saying. "And both horse and griffin are natural beings, so they would not have been affected by the barrier."

Staples rocked his head from side to side. "Well, no, they wouldn't. But that doesn't explain anything. Certainly both animals could have been present at the crucial moment, and it's possible I suppose that the griffin had been trained to attack a human figure, or that Baskerville himself did something to provoke it. And I suppose he might have died of fright because he was convinced that the curse had fallen upon him. But neither the horse nor the griffin could have been magically compelled to enter the grounds because any Spell of Duress or similar form of magic would have been neutralized as soon as they broached the perimeter."

"It seems rather unlikely that this was simply mischance."

"No, it is more likely simple murder, or rather, not so simple murder. The flaw in my theory is that too much of the detail depended upon luck, and a failed first attempt would have put Baskerville on guard against a second. It might also have provided clues leading back to whoever was behind it all." He hesitated. "And there have been other things." Staples repeated a somewhat abridged version of the other encounters about which I had already been told. "And even I have heard strange sounds out in the swamps, particularly at night. I don't like to go out there after dark even under ordinary circumstances, but some of my observations require a nocturnal visit. I am always acutely aware of the fact that if I were to have an accident, it might be a long time before I was found."

"What sort of strange sounds?"

"A kind of thin shrieking is the most common. It lasts for a few seconds, then fades away, as though whatever caused it was receding into the distance. And on two occasions I heard a succession of loud vibrations, as though powerful wings were stirring the air."

"Did you investigate?"

He shook his head. "It's easy enough to get lost out there in the daylight. I wouldn't risk a route I hadn't thoroughly explored in the dark. And frankly, it was none of my business. This all happened before Baskerville was killed, you realize."

"Has anyone else heard these sounds?"

Staples shrugged expressively. "If so, they haven't spoken of it to me. I'm the only one foolish enough to wander into the swamp after darkness, so perhaps not, although sound travels a good distance here at night. The mountains reflect it back, I imagine."

"And you have no idea where they might have originated?"

He scratched his head. "I had the impression that they came from somewhere on the east side of the swamp."

"Is that near the old burial ground I've heard about?"

"No, quite the opposite. I've only been up that way once. There's not much to see and anthropology isn't my line anyway. I don't even recall what tribe it was. There are a bunch of elongated humps in the soil, arranged in a straight line, about a dozen. That's it. No markers, no totem poles or anything like that. There are sinkholes all around that area, which makes it doubly dangerous. No one goes up there any more."

I finished my lemonade and, convinced that I had gleaned all from my companion that he was likely to tell me that day, I took my leave. He walked me to the door and told me to give my regards to Dr. James when I saw him.

But my visit was to be delayed yet again. I had started back across the narrow road when I noticed a woman standing beside the parked car. She was quite elderly, had a slight stoop, and wore a dark scarf wrapped around her hair so that she looked almost like a monk. I nodded in her direction and continued toward the clinic door, but she moved with sudden surprising quickness and intercepted me.

"You're one of the ones from the Manor, aren't you?" Her voice was gravelly but strong.

I reached the curb and stopped. "Yes," I admitted. "I'm Sir Henry's secretary, Perry Everdeen. And you are?"

She ignored my question. "You'd best get back into your car and drive out of this valley and never look back."

Not the most hospitable greeting I'd ever received. "I beg your pardon?"

"The curse will not be denied. It will take the last of the Baskervilles before it's done. And woe unto anyone who stands in the way."

"What do you know about the curse?" I asked.

"I know enough to give it a wide berth. You won't see me inside those gates while there is still a Baskerville drawing breath. I've seen it in the darkness, heard it crying out for vengeance. It's coming, I tell you, and you'd best stand aside before it smites you down."

I'm not sure what I might have said at this point but I was forestalled. Mortimer James came out of his front door. His expression suggested irritation and amusement in equal measure. "What are you saying to our new guest, Mrs. Ardmore? You're not trying to frighten him off with ghost stories, are you?"

There was no confusion of emotion on her face now. She was furious. "I was just warning him, just as I warned you, Mortimer James. Every time you visit that place, you put your mortal life at risk. It's coming just like I always said it would."

"Well, I'll certainly let you know when it arrives. Perhaps you can invite it over for tea, since the two of you are such old acquaintances."

I could almost see steam coming out of her ears now. "You mock me, Mortimer James, but I have powers. I know things that are hidden from the rest of you." She gathered herself together. "But I also know when I'm not wanted." Her head turned and her eyes locked on mine. "Heed my warning, young man. Death will come to Baskerville Manor again, and soon." And then she stalked off.

James sighed heavily. "You have to forgive Mrs. Ardmore. A touch of Alzheimers, I'm afraid."

"Does she really have some kind of second sight?"

"She did have, when she was younger. And she could craft a very effective charm as well. When her mind started to go, her family had to go to court for a Potion of Suppression because her abilities were potentially dangerous, both to herself and others. She still thinks she has visions and premonitions, but they're a product of her imagination now rather than glimpses into the ethereal world." He shook his head sadly. "I noticed the car outside but I didn't see anyone around."

"I was visiting with your neighbor across the way, Mr. Staples."

"Ah, so you've met Dennis."

"Dolores as well."

"Pleasant people, both of them, although Dolores has her dour side. I assume you've come to see me as well. Why don't we go indoors?"

The clinic looked rather rustic on the outside but the interior was very different. The waiting room had only a half dozen seats and was decorated with diagrams of the human body, pyramidal healing spells, a chart of common medicinal herbs, and an illustration of how to perform the Heimlich maneuver. There was a bell and a receptionist cubicle, but no receptionist.

"One of the Daimler girls comes in a couple of times a week to take care of my paperwork, but we're pretty informal out here. And the local folk are generally quite healthy. I sometimes go a full week without a single patient. I make more money writing papers for the medical and esoteric journals than I do from my practice."

There were only two treatment rooms and they were mirror images of each other. James had a small office at the rear, near a staircase that led to the second floor. "We live upstairs and in back. It's small but it suits us. I'd introduce you to my wife but she drove down south to pick up a few things we can't get in the valley."

I sat in one of two guest chairs while James went behind the desk. "Settling in all right up at the Manor?"

"Pretty much. Sir Henry seems satisfied. Did you know that the Lionels were planning to leave?"

James looked uncomfortable. "They never said anything but they've both been acting a little oddly since Charles died. I assumed they were frightened and that could be the case, but it might just be that they figure they're too old to adapt to a new master. They'd been with Charles for nearly thirty years."

"Did anything else happen here while you were gone?"

"Not that I have heard. Mrs. Vaughn was in this morning and she soaks up the local gossip like a sponge. Near talked my ear before I could get rid of her but none of it had anything to do with the Manor except that one of the village girls who works there occasionally got pregnant and ran off with her boyfriend." He sighed. "Most of the young people can't wait to move away from the valley. The lure of the city and all that. And to be fair, we don't have much here to keep them entertained."

I told him about my conversation with Wanda. "So I'm going to be on my own for a while. You do know that I'm not really a detective, don't you?"

"I'm sure you'll do your best for us."

"Let's hope it's enough."

We talked for a few more minutes and Dr. James promised to check in at the Manor regularly, but neither of us gained any real sense of confidence that things were under control.

I let myself out, but I was not destined to return to the Manor quite yet. Dolores was waiting for me and she hailed me from across the street.

"I saw you talking to Mrs. Ardmore earlier. I assume she wasn't welcoming you to the valley."

"No, she was warning me off actually. It's all right. Mortimer explained that she was senile."

"She is that, true enough, but that doesn't mean she wasn't talking sense. Oh, I know that they supposedly took her magic away because she wasn't responsible any more, but the sight has a way of persisting. I might not believe everything she told me, but I wouldn't ignore it either. If you have any influence with Henry Baskerville, you should use it to convince him to go home."

And she turned and went back inside.

CHAPTER TEN

After picking up a few items at the drug store, I drove back to the Manor. I considered describing my little adventure to Sir Henry, but he hadn't left the library and when I peeked inside, he seemed to be asleep in his chair. Upon reflection I decided that I was not going to be turned into a messenger between the local people and Sir Henry unless it suited my own purposes and that if they had anything to say to him, they could do it directly. Julia tells me that I have a stubborn streak and she is probably right, as she is about most things.

I had heard a radio report about the escaped convict during the trip back. The authorities were now reasonably certain that he had left the valley, but they stopped short of actually telling the residents that they could leave doors and windows unlocked again. The fact that he continued to evade them seemed to me proof that they could not be as sure of themselves as they claimed and perhaps they were hoping that word of their conviction would get back to him and lure him out of cover.

I used the report as an opening to start a conversation with Lionel, hoping to draw him out on other subjects, but he was almost the caricature of a reticent professional servant. He answered direct questions, never contradicted me even by so much as a raised eyebrow, and never volunteered an opinion of his own. When I asked what people thought of Mr. Staples, he said that he'd never heard a word of complaint, that his cousin had been born and brought up in the valley, and that he had never ventured into the swamps himself and believed them to be quite dangerous. He deemed Mrs. Ardmore "a poor soul" and confirmed that she had possessed a remarkable degree of second sight when she was younger. "All of that is past now," I'm afraid.

Rebuffed there, I went to the kitchen, supposedly in search of something cool to drink, but Mrs. Lionel was even more close mouthed than her husband and was so obviously ill at ease with my presence in her private domain that I took pity on her and went for a walk.

The gardeners were making quick work of it. One of their trucks was already filled with trimmings and fallen branches, much of the garden showed visible signs of skilled care, and they were busily engaged in digging out an old stump when I passed. There was no opportunity to start a conversation there either, so I turned toward the garage – which had quite obviously begun life as a stable – in search of Billy, the painter.

He was cleaning his brushes when I came upon him. The entire rear wall now sported a fresh coat of gray paint. He'd been very careful and I saw no dripping or spattering on the white trim. I complimented him on his care and he thanked me.

"I'm always careful in my work. My father used to tell me that the most valuable tool a handyman could carry was a good reputation."

"That's true of every profession," I replied. "But nevertheless somewhat rare. Have you done much work here in the past?"

"The old Mr. Baskerville was my best customer. I hope the same may be true of the new one. I clean out the gutters every spring and wash the outside of all the windows twice a year. Last year I repaired one of the chimneys and I helped Mrs. Lionel when she was having trouble with plumbing in the kitchen the year before that. I mend furniture, rake leaves, and even do a little electrical work. Most electricians nowadays have a basilisk or a set of spells, but none of that works inside the Manor."

"What kind of man was Charles Baskerville? The Lionels seem to have been devoted to him."

"He was a very good man. He paid a fair wage, helped out when someone needed it, and did a lot to build up the village. The new man has some big shoes to fill."

"Henry seems a good enough fellow. I don't think you'll have much to complain of." I decided to take a chance. "I gather some of the local people think that the family curse was at fault."

"There's some that thinks that way and others that don't. The curse was supposed to punish the evil, and Mr. Baskerville was a good man. And magic doesn't work up here."

"So do you think he was murdered?"

Billy wasn't willing to go that far. "Why would anyone want to kill him? There was nothing to steal and he didn't have any enemies that anyone ever heard of. He almost never left the valley, at least these last ten years, so someone would have known about it, wouldn't they? I think something attacked him, some animal, and he took fright and started to run and his heart gave out. That's what they said it was that killed him, his heart."

"But what kind of animal would attack a man and claw his face but disappear without leaving a trace?"

Billy wasn't willing to speculate any further though. "There's lots of dangerous animals in the world. Maybe something wandered into the valley and is hiding out in the swamps, and maybe it was out that night and Mr. Baskerville frightened it. Almost no one ever goes into the swamp, except Mr. Staples, and I think the man's daft. There are sinkholes and overgrown ravines and all sorts of things out there. Even when I was a kid, we'd never go any deeper than just around the edges."

Billy had finished cleaning his brushes and I helped him carry them and the leftover paint to a little wooden shed that was so overgrown that I hadn't seen it until he pointed it out. He was clearly impatient to go so I complimented his work once more and took my leave.

Sir Henry and Lionel were just coming out of the front door when I made my way back around the end of the Manor. The former beckoned for me to join them. "Lionel is going to show us where it happened." I had already gone over the ground based on the description we'd already been provided and I had a pretty good picture in my head, but I acquiesced without mentioning that.

The low wall ended near the gravel road so it was easy enough to determine where Charles Baskerville had cleaned out his pipe and smoked a fresh one. "He was lying face down over there," said Lionel as he pointed toward an open patch of lawn not far from an ornamental shrub. "I didn't notice the wounds on his face until I had him inside. It was very dark that night, not much moon and what there was covered by cloud. I was quite sure that he was dead already, but I couldn't just leave him lying there on the cold ground."

"And no one heard anything?"

"Not a sound, sir. But it would have to have been quite loud. My wife was busy in the kitchen at the rear of the house and I was in the attic. Sir Henry had boxed up some old household goods and asked me to store them there out of the way."

"Had he been acting oddly in the days before his death?" I asked.

"It would be inappropriate for me to make a judgment about the nature of his actions, but he had seemed somewhat disturbed. There had been some unusual sounds in the night."

"What kind of sounds?" I asked, anticipating Sir Henry.

"The calling of some sort of animal, or at least that was what we thought it was."

"Then you heard it too?"

"Oh, yes. On two occasions. Both times at night and both times while I was with Mr. Charles. They never lasted more than a few seconds."

"Were you able to determine where the sounds originated?" asked Sir Henry.

"No, sir. They never lasted long enough to be helpful. On the first occasion they were quite distant, but the second time I was certain that whatever the source of the disturbance might be, it was closer than the small gate. Sir Charles and I actually walked the grounds on that occasion, but we learned nothing by it."

Our supper that evening was the best prepared piece of salmon that I have ever eaten. Mrs. Lionel even sketched a smile when Sir Henry praised it loudly. We retired to the den with a fresh bottle of brandy – Sir Henry was obviously quite fond of his drink – and I sipped at mine while he finished three snifters. He asked me a few questions about Wanda and I answered them as politically as I could and without revealing any confidential information. I assured him that she was the best private investigator in New England and that he could be assured that she would do her best for him.

When he realized that I was not going to regale him with exciting or titillating details of past cases, he lapsed into silence and it was my turn to choose the topic. I asked about the Baskerville family curse.

"Well, it was long before my time, obviously, and had been nullified before I was born. It was almost certainly genuine though perhaps not very specific and my disreputable ancestor who caused its creation well deserved his unsavory death. It was supposed to punish only those who deserved retribution – which was rather more discriminating than most family curses are reputed to be – and some of those who fell to it were clearly not pillars of the community. At least two seemed to be praiseworthy folk – one was a vicar – but of course they could have been guilty of secret sins."

"Do you think your uncle fell into that category?"

"I wish that I could express an opinion on the subject, but except for occasional letters which were frankly not very personal, we had no intercourse. I had never met my uncle and only spoke to him once, through a clairvoyant, when he delivered his condolences on the death of my father."

There was a bit more conversation after that but neither of us learned anything of interest and when I finished my brandy, I discovered that I was feeling sleepy and took my leave. He was refilling his snifter as I walked out the door.

Dr. James brought two of the local people for lunch at the Manor the following day in order to begin the process of introducing Sir Henry to his new neighbors. One of them was Dennis Staples, whom I had already met. The other was Frank Lafter, a retired lawyer who had found a new vocation as a farmer, or more properly as a farm administrator since he was not young enough to do much of the actual physical work and had not led a lifestyle conducive to such exertion. The other farmers, according to James, held him in an esteem that had been second only to Charles Baskerville, and if there was such a thing as a spokesperson for the tenants, Lafter filled that role.

"The nearest municipal court is way down south in Montpelier, so when there is a local dispute, it is often referred to me first. I can usually explain to the parties how a judge is likely to rule and if we can work out a compromise ourselves, it saves them the trouble and expense of taking formal legal action."

"Is there a lot of that sort of thing?" inquired Sir Henry.

"Not at all, and mostly it's minor squabbles. A dog will kill a neighbor's chicken or a fertility spell will spill over from one farm to the next and interfere with a field left fallow or something along those lines. There were two families who feuded for some time over some silly argument but the Travises moved away a while back and Abner Fox has mellowed with age. No, you'll find this to be a peaceful community. Some might call it boring."

"I was told that the younger people in the area tended to move away," I interposed.

"There's a good deal of truth in that. I know that Calvin Roberts is upset that neither of his boys wants to be a farmer. You can't really blame them. Hiram Anderson is the most prosperous among us, and he hardly leads a life of leisure. The big farms out west with golem workers have set the prices so low that the chain stores don't even bother with us anymore. Most of my own crop goes to restaurants in Burlington and I run a little roadside stand in Morristown that does pretty well. I take stuff from my neighbors up there as well."

Lafter was also an amateur astrologer. "I have a little telescope mounted on the roof of the house in a kind of widow's walk. I keep charts and try to match them against the professional predictions in the newspaper. I can't say I measure up very well. I was up there the last couple of nights, in fact, but for a different reason. You've heard about our escaped convict, I assume."

We admitted that we had.

"Well, I've never been convinced that the police are telling us everything they know. Hell, I worked in criminal law for thirty years and I know damned well they hold things back. So I've been using the telescope nights to look for signs that the man is still in the area."

Sir Henry raised an eyebrow. "Do you really think so?"

"I think it's possible."

I stirred myself. "But what could you see at night? I mean, once it's dark, someone could move around the valley and be virtually invisible, couldn't they?"

"If they were just walking about that would be correct. Now if I was trying to elude the authorities, I'd be hidden away in the swamps, probably someplace where I had alternate escape routes if I heard anyone coming. There's been some food gone missing the last few days. Someone took eggs from the Gilberts' henhouse, a loaf of bread disappeared from Emily Rhodes' kitchen – though she thinks her brother might have taken it with him when he left to hike in the mountains, and it wouldn't be hard to dig up some carrots, potatoes, and suchlike without making it obvious."

He paused to take a sip of lemonade. "But you see, our nights are still pretty chilly. And why eat raw vegetables when you can cook them? So if I were hiding out, I'd also make sure I was well shielded from view and I'd light a fire at night. During the day the smoke would be a dead giveaway, of course, but at night you could build a comfortable one and sleep beside it. I thought I might be able to spot the light with my telescope, but I'm afraid even the roof of my house isn't high enough." He glanced around. "From up here, you'd have a much better chance, Sir Henry."

"Undoubtedly. But is your instrument portable?"

"Unfortunately, no, or at least not without considerable effort. I wasn't seriously suggesting such a course. And after all, the police might be perfectly correct that the fugitive has fled from the valley. And if not, he will surely do so soon."

Our guests departed soon afterward and I retired to my room. Since I was unable to call Wanda with my latest discoveries, tenuous though they may be, I began to set down detailed notes of everything that had happened since our arrival, using the notebook which I had purchased the previous day. I had not expected this to take very long, but once I started, I realized that I had learned a great deal in a very short period of time, although none of it seemed likely to help us solve the mystery of the death of Charles Baskerville.

CHAPTER ELEVEN

When I had finished, I went back downstairs where I learned that Sir Henry had taken the car and gone into the village. I was a bit concerned about this because Wanda had told me to keep as close a watch on him as was practical. Although she hadn't said so directly, I suspected that she feared that he might be in danger of the same fate that had struck down his uncle, whether it be human or supernormal. I was uneasy with the thought of him wandering alone unattended.

The last of the gardeners had finished up during the morning, so I found myself alone at the Manor with just the Lionels. When he mentioned that he was going out to inspect the work in the garden, I decided to make a second attempt at drawing Mrs. Lionel out, but she was not in the kitchen when I looked there and a quick tour of the ground floor was unproductive.

Curious, I used the staircase and was just about to look into the library when I saw her come from the direction of Sir Henry's bedroom with a laundry bundle in her arms. She hesitated just for a second when she saw me, her face betraying nothing, and as she passed on her way downstairs she murmured something about checking to see that Sir Henry had fresh towels in his bath. That would have been quite a reasonable explanation had it not been for the fact that I had seen her replacing the towels earlier in the morning. There was no possible reason for her to have done so again since Sir Henry had not likely bathed after lunch. If she was just taking his dirty clothes to be washed, why would she lie about it?

My interest in the Lionels grew stronger, but I could not at present see any means by which I could satisfy my curiosity. I stood bemused for a minute or two, then descended, intending to revive my attempt to beard her in her own lair, but the kitchen remained unoccupied and through the window I saw her in the garden, talking to her husband. She seemed agitated and I thought he was attempting to calm her. They turned and walked behind a row of poplars and I lost sight of them.

Sir Henry returned a short time later. He volunteered nothing about his trip to the village and I didn't ask. This was the first day upon which I was actually called upon to function as his secretary, for he had a good number of business matters to contend with. I took some dictation and later typed up several letters – there was a quite modern ABM typewriter in the library – and we sorted through an entire filing cabinet which Charles Baskerville had kept in meticulous order. These contained all of the leases on the farms as well as the deeds to what was virtually the entire valley. Sir Henry now owned everything within the mountains except for the village of Grimalkin proper and two farms at the northern end which had been sold off some time in the past. There was a ledger listing payments from the tenants, and I noticed that they were periods during which one or more of them had been technically delinquent for an extended period of time. None of them had been charged interest or any other penalty insofar as I could determine and all had eventually made good their debts.

There were several folders of miscellaneous legal papers – tax records, reports from the Ethereal Protective Agency, official plot surveys, insurance certificates, and various contracts including an annual levee for the suppression spell that protected the Manor from magical intrusions. I recognized the firm that had done the conjuration. They had an enviable reputation. There were multiple copies of Charles' last will and testament and the financial covenants establishing the retirement trust for the Lionels.

There was almost nothing personal in the paperwork I reviewed, and no mention whatsoever of the family curse. Everything appeared to be in order and complete.

We had another splendid meal that evening but I thought that Mrs. Lionel was even more subdued than normal. Sir Henry reluctantly set the brandy aside after a single drink and asked me to follow him to the library. A second session of paperwork, dictation, and typing followed. This time we were concerned solely with his holdings in England. There was correspondence with the bank that held the mortgage, with two different preservation societies, with the firm that managed Sir Henry's investment portfolio, and with a handful of creditors. I judged his financial position overall to be precarious, but not desperate. He told me quite frankly that it had been a constant struggle to keep his head above water.

"I've never actually defaulted on a payment, but it has been close at times. I have to admit that my uncle's death came at an opportune time."

I asked if he had made a decision about his long term plans. He was obviously committed to keeping Baskerville Hall in the family, and certainly must be less attached to the Manor.

"I'll have to see how life here suits me. I could let out the Hall. It's been well maintained and it's rather more than I need. The servant wing alone is nearly as large as the Manor. I feel an obligation to keep it in the family, but not necessarily as my own residence."

At last we were finished, as much as paperwork is ever really finished. Sir Henry had another bottle of brandy in the library and I joined him for one drink, then retired for the night, adding some brief notes to my summary before taking to my bed.

Normally I am a very sound sleeper. Julia jokes that the Four Horsemen could ride through our bedroom without rousing me. But for some reason I found myself wide awake and with my eyes open just after two in the morning. Something had disturbed my rest, presumably some sound although I heard nothing at that moment. The conviction was so strong that I slipped quietly out of bed and put on my robe.

No lights were kept lit after dark at the Manor but I had not drawn the curtains and the clouds had finally thinned enough that the moonlight was able to break through. Barefoot, I walked to the door, which I had not locked, and slowly turned the knob until I could ease it open.

I began to feel foolish when I stuck my head out into the hallway. There did not seem to be anyone about and I certainly couldn't hear anything out of the ordinary. I told myself that I was being silly and was about to go back to bed when the faintest hint of a shifting of shadows, perhaps accompanied by a sound so low that I didn't consciously hear it, froze me in place. Someone or something was moving at the far end of the hallway.

Rather than investigate proactively, I drew back, closing the door so that I could just see through the opening. Without a light at my back, I was confident that I was effectively invisible. As I watched, my eyes adjusted enough that I could make out the general shape. It was a human figure, too tall to be either Sir Henry or Mrs. Lionel, so it had to be her husband, unless some intruder had somehow managed to break into the house.

The shadow disappeared around the far corner and I carefully stepped out of my room, took a deep breath, and tiptoed until I reached the spot where I had last seen the shape. There were two bedrooms and another bath further along, and then the hall came to an abrupt end at a window. The hallway itself was empty when I cautiously peered around the corner, so obviously Lionel – if that's who it had been – must have gone into one of the three rooms. The doors were all open but none of the lights were on although, after a moment, I saw a faint glow from the nearest. I guessed that it was either a flashlight or a luminous charm, then realized it had to be the former because a charm would not have worked.

He stayed there for several minutes and once I thought I heard him speaking, presumably to himself because the room – when I entered it a short time later – was completely empty. When the light went off, I quickly retreated to my own room, closing the door just in time. As the dark figure passed, I confirmed what I already suspected. It was Lionel, walking stealthily and with his head down. He passed close enough that I might have reached out and touched him, but he never looked in my direction.

When I knew that he was descending the staircase, I left my room, still moving as quietly as possible. No one else could have passed me from the end of the hall, so I investigated cautiously. The room which Lionel visited contained furniture very similar to that in my own, but there were no living inhabitants and nothing unusual to suggest any hidden motive. I went to the window and looked down onto the grounds, but that was similarly uninformative. Just to be thorough, I checked the second bedroom and the common bath, but everything was as it should have been.

I was puzzled and perhaps even a little bit alarmed, and I could not conceive of any rational reason for the nocturnal visit. But I was quite sure that Lionel was not walking in his sleep, checking to see that the windows were secured, or engaging in any other reputable business.

It was a while before I could get back to sleep and I used that time to update my notes. I also took pains to conceal the notebook under a cushion on one of the chairs rather than leave it on the desk. I would not have put it past either of the Lionels to read it during my absence.

I would like to say that the rest of the night passed without incident, but there was one more event that troubled my sleep. Once again I am not certain what it was that disturbed me, but about two hours later, I found myself awake again. This time there was no sense of alarm or intrusion, but I was restless and made a trip to the bathroom. The house was so quiet that I could hear the grandfather clock ticking at the foot of the staircase.

Although my body ached for repose, my mind was churning and when I returned to my room I went over to the window. It was fully dark but the clouds had almost completely dissipated during the night. The moon was three quarters full and had the faintest bluish tinge, which is supposed to be a sign that something significant was about to happen. I had started to turn back toward my bed when I noticed something out of place.

I mentioned earlier that the window in my room looked down across an extent of grass that ended at the edge of the small cemetery. There was an entranceway flanked by two large shrubs. To one side, a life sized statue of an angle stood with one hand inclined toward the entrance, as though inviting visitors to enter. The statue was exactly as it had always been, but there was a second human figure standing behind it, just visible from the angle afforded me.

At first I thought it just a shadow and I might still have turned away had it not moved suddenly and purposefully. It was so quick that I missed my only chance to identify what I saw, but it was clearly human, about average height, and wearing some sort of dark, heavy coat or cloak. It passed into the cemetery and out of my sight before I could note anything else.

I was quite certain that this was not Lionel, who was both taller and somewhat sturdier. Nor could it have been his wife or Sir Henry, both of whom were shorter and/or heavier. Whoever it was clearly did not belong and was taking pains not to chance being seen, even though it was unlikely that anyone would be about at this hour of the morning.

Although I considered rousing Lionel, I decided against it. He and Sir Henry might well dismiss it as a trick of the night, shadow with no substance. I knew otherwise, but in the absence of other evidence, I wasn't sure that I could present a convincing case. But neither could I sit around and do nothing, and there was no question at this point of going back to bed.

So I dressed myself and went quietly downstairs. I took one of the spare keys from the rack in the butler's pantry and let myself out of back door of the Manor, locking it behind me. It was cool but surprisingly light outside. The moon was apparently determined to make up for lost time.

I stayed close to the Manor wall as I made my way around the side, hoping not to present a detectible silhouette, and naturally I made as little noise as possible. At the end of the wall, I studied the cemetery from a distance, but there was no movement there now, no sign of an intruder. It occurred to me that I might have taken a poker from the fireplace to serve as a weapon, but I wasn't about to go back for it now. I glanced around but nothing suggested itself, so I took my nerve into my hands and started across the grass.

When I passed between the two shrubs, I was greeted with quite literally the silence of the graveyard. There were about thirty grave markers – all of the Baskervilles from this branch of the family had been laid to rest here. Charles himself was toward the rear. His will had specified a plain stone marker. There was still a slight swell in the ground where he had been buried, but it would subside quickly now that the ground had thawed.

Except for a few attenuated poplars, there was nothing large enough to conceal even the smallest of lurking figures. The cemetery was bounded on three sides by a low cut hedge, but any but the smallest of children could have jumped over them readily enough. But I hadn't imagined the figure I had seen. When I knelt just inside the entrance, I saw where a footprint had been pressed into the dewy grass, and it faded even while I was staring at it.

CHAPTER TWELVE

Lionel seemed as staid as always at breakfast the next morning and his wife was similarly unchanged. I refrained from mentioning either of my odd experiences of the night before until they were both absent, then gave Sir Henry a brief summary of events, speaking in a low voice so that I could not be overheard.

Sir Henry was not as surprised in the first instance as I had expected. "I couldn't sleep two nights back and went to the library for some brandy. Lionel was walking about at the time and claimed that he thought he'd heard someone call out and had come upstairs to investigate. I thought he looked a bit guilty at the time, but I'd forgotten all about it until just now."

The trespasser in the cemetery seemed of more interest. "Did you get a good look at the fellow?"

"I'm afraid not. He was just there for a second and it was dark."

"I can't imagine what he'd find of interest among the graves."

"Perhaps that wasn't his object. He might have been on the grounds for some considerable time before I spotted him." But I doubted that he had remained afterward because I'd had a thorough look around before going back inside.

I was rather more interested in Lionel. "It sounds as though he might make a habit of prowling around at night."

"Twice is hardly a habit," Sir Henry objected.

"Twice in three nights," I pointed out. "And he may have been about on the third as well."

"I'll call him in and demand an explanation."

But I talked him out of it. "There is nothing with which we can compel him to tell us the truth. I think we need to consider another option." I suggested that we adopt stealth of our own and attempt to determine just what it was that Lionel was watching from the window of the unused bedroom.

After breakfast, we went for a walk, ostensibly for exercise but primarily to examine the swath of ground which was immediately visible from Lionel's secretive surveillance point. The lawn was foreshortened on that side of the house and a fairly dense stand of unruly trees appeared to present a nearly impenetrable barrier. But appearances were misleading. Once we were close enough, there was a noticeable gap which, we discovered, was the beginning of a narrow but well traveled path.

"Where do you suppose it leads?" asked Sir Henry.

"Shall we find out for ourselves?" And so it was that the two of us moved single file into the woods.

We spoke very little as we followed the winding trail over a gentle hump, after which it descended quite rapidly, roughly paralleling the line of mountains to the east. Twenty minutes later I was completely disoriented – I am city born and bred – but Sir Henry ventured the theory that we were headed toward the southern swampland. His opinion proved to be accurate for ten minutes later we emerged into a cleared space that overlooked a rather dismal stretch of land. The trail continued downward more steeply at this point, but the footing looked treacherous. The air carried a fetid smell that was most unpleasant, and we could see where the solid ground gradually gave way to greasy mud and small pools of water.

"I don't fancy going any further without a pair of rubber boots," said Sir Henry, and I found myself agreeing with him. In any case, the mystery of Lionel's nightly vigils seemed no closer to a solution than when we had started. We didn't even have firm reason to believe that this trail had anything to do with the object of his surveillance.

It was uphill all of the way back and I was quite winded upon arriving. Vigorous exercise is not one of my habits. Sir Henry was in good spirits, however, and clearly in better shape than I was despite the difference in our ages. I went inside, promising to complete the filing I had left undone the night before, but my companion announced his intention of walking down to the large gate and back. "I'm not one for paperwork, as you might have guessed. This enforced inactivity is not good for me and I'm restless." And off he went while I marveled at his stamina.

That afternoon, I discovered that Sir Henry had a secret of his own. He took the car into Grimalkin again without mentioning to me that he was going. Of course he was not accountable by any means, but part of the reason that I was posing as his employee was for his personal protection. Although we had no specific reason to believe that whatever had struck down his uncle might claim him as its next victim, it was certainly within the realm of possibility, and there was definitely ample reason to believe that he might be at risk.

Since I could obviously not compel him to provide an explanation – and upon his return two hours later he did not volunteer one – I was both puzzled and mildly annoyed. We worked our way through some more of his uncle's papers that afternoon – mostly random correspondence which most people would long since have discarded – but I made a point of reading everything on the chance that some clue to his fate might be contained there. Except for some letters relating to a farmer whom he had evicted ten years earlier, there was nothing even hinting of conflict. The dispossessed farmer, I learned later, had died of a stroke a few years later.

I was feeling rather dispirited by the time we ate and Sir Henry had been quieter than usual since his return, so I asked if I might borrow the car for an hour or two. "A touch of cabin fever," I explained. "I understand one of the local bars has a pool table." In fact, I'd seen a neon sign advertising that fact.

"Pool? Oh, you mean billiards." Sir Henry seemed only mildly interested. "Never had time for games myself. But go right ahead, Mr. Everdeen. I'm for a glass of brandy and perhaps an early night. Don't stay out too late."

That reminded me that we had agreed to keep an eye out for Lionel that night. "I won't be late, but I'll take a key just in case."

The Black Goat Tavern was nicer on the inside than the exterior might suggest. It was rather lavishly furnished, in fact, and considerably larger than I had realized. It could easily have accommodated fifty customers, although there were only half a dozen when I arrived. It was, after all, a week night, and this was a farming community in the midst of spring planting. There was, indeed, a pool table, but it was not in use and I hadn't actually come looking for a game in any case. It was information that I was after.

I received a few curious but not unfriendly glances when I walked in. The bartender was a young woman with a hard look about her, although she was friendly enough when she took my order. "Passing through?"

I explained that I was staying at the Manor, working for the new owner.

"Your boss was in earlier today. I hope you'll both turn out to be regular customers. We could do with the business."

I said something to the effect that Sir Henry was probably making an effort to meet the local people although truthfully I was rather surprised to learn that he'd preceded me. I confess I found him a bit stuffy. Perhaps he had thought this was the closest he could find to a friendly pub.

The bartender, who introduced herself as Liz, was doubtful. "He didn't seem inclined to talk to anyone except the woman who met him here."

I couldn't imagine how Sir Henry had found time to strike up an acquaintance since he'd hardly been out of my sight since we'd arrived. "I didn't know he'd met any of the local women. We've only been in the valley for a few days."

"Wasn't a local. Never saw her before. She came in maybe a quarter hour before he did and used the public phone. Then she ordered coffee and a sandwich and sat in a booth in the back. When he came in, he was obviously looking for her. I brought him a brandy when he asked and another when I went to see if they needed anything. They didn't act like strangers."

"Maybe it was someone passing through whom he'd met before." But Sir Henry had said that he'd never been in the States before. "Did she have an accent like his?"

"Not that I noticed."

Three more customers came in and Liz moved to serve them. I made an attempt to start a conversation with a pair of obvious farmhands who were drinking beer but we had so little in common that I felt that I was drawing attention to myself and moved on. I could think of no excuse to address the occupants of two booths and another party – two middle aged couples – was caught up in family reminiscences.

The newcomers were considerably younger – two men and a rather plain looking young woman – and they were more interested in the fantasy football game on the oversized television mounted above the bar. The Cincinnati Centaurs were playing the Oregon Ogres in the semi-finals. They were friendly enough when I joined them, but their conversational skills were limited.

I allowed Liz to freshen my drink even though I really didn't want any more. It would have looked strange if I had just carried an empty glass around. "It's not very lively tonight, is it?" I asked.

"Saturdays are better, but the last time we were actually busy was New Year's."

"Yet you have two bars in town."

She laughed shortly. "Not really. Chloe's Wine and Spirits is mostly for fortune telling and séances. Chloe took the bar out when her mother was declared incompetent."

"Would that be Mrs. Ardmore?"

"It would indeed. Have you met the lady?"

"Yes I have. She uttered dire warnings and suggested that I leave town."

Liz nodded. "She was always funny about the Manor. Told Charles Baskerville he should burn it down, sell off the property, and move somewhere else. And that was before her mind started to go. But maybe she did pick up on something. He's dead, after all, and not from natural causes either."

I wanted to talk to her longer, but another handful of customers arrived, and the Centaur fans all wanted refills, and I finally got discouraged, waved a goodbye, left a nice tip which I added to my expense account, and drove back to the Manor.

Sir Henry was in the library. I was tempted to make an offhand comment about his meeting with the unknown woman, but I couldn't think of a way to bring up the subject without sounding as though I was spying on him, which really wasn't the case although I now had another mysterious incident to record in my notes. He offered me a drink which I declined. His capacity for alcohol was enormous and since he couldn't possibly be using an anti-intoxication charm, it had to be natural. For his part he showed no interest in what I had been doing in the village and I didn't offer to enlighten him.

"How are we going to go about watching our nocturnal butler?" I asked.

"We'll retire at our usual time and make sure he's aware of it. Wait in your room for half an hour, then come across to mine. I'll leave the door unlocked so don't knock. I have some candles – we don't want to show a light. I doubt that he can pass by my door without being heard now that we know what to listen for."

We had almost given up our vigil when we were finally rewarded. I was on the verge of nodding off at the time – it was well past midnight – but Sir Henry suddenly stirred and I raised my head just in time to hear what was undoubtedly a cautious footstep just outside the door. We waited tensely for the next, which came after a short interval, and another followed that. By the time they were far enough away that we were confident Lionel had reached the bend in the corridor, we were both standing by the door. I can't speak for Sir Henry but my heart was racing.

Sir Henry opened the door very slowly and peered around the edge, then stepped lightly out into the corridor. For such a solid man, he moved with surprising agility and I doubt he made as much noise as had Lionel moments before. I did my best to emulate his care and we were soon standing side by side in the hallway.

One cautious step at a time, we followed in Lionel's path until we also had reached the bend. Once again Sir Henry scouted carefully ahead, then beckoned for me to follow. We rounded the corner and saw a shadowy but empty stretch of carpeting. From one of the open doors – the same I had visited previously – there was the faintest hint of light.

Sir Henry indicated that I should move ahead and I passed the door as quickly as possible, pausing on the opposite side. The two of us then acted in unison, craning our heads past the door jambs so that we could look into the room.

Lionel was standing with his face pressed close to the window. He held a flashlight in one hand, but his arms were at his sides and it was pointed at the floor near his feet. Even had the room been fully illuminated we could not have appraised his expression because he was facing away from us.

I had decided that the only way to plumb this mystery was through confrontation and apparently Sir Henry had reached the same conclusion. After barely a half minute or so had passed, he stepped forward boldly and entered the room.

"Lionel! What the devil are you doing up here at this time of the night?"

The butler had drawn back so violently that I steeled myself for a fight if it was necessary. But it was shock rather than anger. "I'm sorry if I have disturbed you, sir. I simply came up to ensure that the windows were all secured. I am in the habit of doing so every evening, just before I retire for the night."

"We're on the second floor, Lionel, and no one is staying in this room. There is no reason why it should have been unlocked."

There was a note of uncertainty in Lionel's voice, but he repeated his claim that it was part of his normal routine.

"That's utter nonsense, man. Tell us the truth now. I insist upon it. What were you watching for outside that window?"

Lionel seemed to shiver and somehow looked smaller than he had. "I can't tell you, sir. It is no threat to you or this house, but it is a secret which I cannot divulge. I'm very sorry, but I cannot."

CHAPTER TWELVE

Sir Henry was not pleased. He clearly was not in the habit of being denied anything by his subordinates. "That will not do, Lionel. I cannot very well have secrets kept from me in my own house. I insist upon an explanation." His voice had grown quite loud.

Lionel drew himself upright and stood stiffly. "I deeply regret that I cannot enlighten you, sir."

I had crossed the room and was glancing out the window when I saw a blinking light appear at what I fancied was the very place where the pathway pierced the line of trees. "He was signaling to someone with the flashlight," I said. "And someone out there is answering with a light of his own."

Sir Henry joined me at the window, but even as he did so, the light blinked off and did not return. I could almost feel the anger pouring off my companion as he turned again toward Lionel. "Who is out there and what business is there between the two of you?"

"I have already told you as much as I can say." His voice quavered. "It is not my secret to divulge, sir. As painful as it is to disobey, it would be dishonorable of me to reveal it."

I'm not sure how Sir Henry might have responded to that because we were interrupted at that point by the arrival of Mrs. Lionel, who was quite literally wringing her hands in dismay.

"It is not my husband's fault," she insisted tearfully. "I made him swear not to tell a living soul."

Put off his guard by this flank attack, Sir Henry modulated his tone. "I can see that you are upset by all of this, Mrs. Lionel, but I'm afraid I must insist on knowing what is going on. This is my home, after all, and there is no room for clandestine meetings and mysterious comings and goings."

And that was when I had one of my rare moments of inspiration because I suddenly realized who was lurking in the woods outside. "It's the escaped convict, isn't it? You're signaling to Selden."

Mrs. Lionel staggered and might have fallen if her husband hadn't hastily taken her by the arm to steady her. "Yes," she admitted in a small voice. "That's my brother Ricky out there."

Sir Henry seemed to be uncharacteristically bereft of words. "Why on Earth would you be signaling to an escaped murderer?"

95

"But he's not a murderer, sir. I know that they found him guilty, but he didn't have a good lawyer and his reputation wasn't the best and his looks argued against him."

Her husband's resistance had also collapsed. "We've been leaving out packets of food and suchlike for him. Only food that we would have thrown out otherwise, sir. And Mrs. Lionel took him a parcel of your uncle's old clothing that would have been thrown out otherwise. You have not suffered in any way from our actions. And we brought him some matches for a fire and an old blanket from the garage since he's been sleeping out in the swamps these last few nights."

Sir Henry stirred himself. "But I don't understand. What's your connection to the man?"

Mrs. Lionel sniffed. "He's my brother, sir. We were orphaned when I was twelve and he was ten and they split us up, sent us to different foster homes. We didn't see each other for years at a time, but I always wrote to him regular and sometimes he even wrote back. It was hard because they moved us around a good deal, but he was always my little brother and I felt responsible for him. He's been in trouble with the law before now but it was always little things – vandalism, shoplifting, purse snatching. He was never violent though, and I know that he didn't kill that man."

I wasn't sure what to expect. Sir Henry struck me as upright and conventional, perhaps even slightly priggish, and I half expected him to call the police immediately. Instead he was silent for so long that the rest of us began to stir nervously.

"I won't make a decision on this matter tonight. Continue with whatever arrangement you had for this evening regarding our...guest. We will speak of this again tomorrow."

Mrs. Lionel thanked Sir Henry profusely and hurried away. Lionel himself hesitated, as though he wished to add something, but then just turned and followed.

"That was hardly what I expected to learn tonight," I ventured.

"It's all rather awkward though. I don't like diddling with the law, or condoning such behavior in others, particularly servants. On the other hand, I of all people should understand that we sometimes do things that fall outside the rules when matters of family are involved. I can't entirely blame the woman for wanting to help her brother, or the man for being loyal to his wife's wishes."

"But on the other hand, Selden is in fact a convicted murderer."

"But not, perhaps, a guilty one." He shook his head. "This is all too convoluted to think about at this ungodly hour. I am for bed."

When I returned to my own room a few minutes later, my thoughts were so abuzz that I thought I would find it impossible to go to sleep, but in fact I was unconscious almost the second my head touched the pillow.

Despite Sir Henry's proclamation, nothing was said about the convict the following morning, or indeed through much of the day. Mrs. Lionel looked more distracted than usual but the butler was very much his normal self, at least outwardly.

We spent much of the day in the library, going through the last of Charles Baskerville's papers. This was a mixed lot including family photographs going back several generations, each annotated on the reverse side, old lease agreements no longer in force, drawings, estimates, and bills for the reconstruction of the stable as a garage, and other materials that were of little value. In none of this did I find anything remotely connected to the Baskerville family curse. Sir Henry sorted the photographs and a few other items that he had decided to retain, but the rest was sentenced to feed the Manor's furnace.

"I have come to a decision regarding our visitor from the swamp." He said the words so casually that it was a second or two before I realized he was referring to Selden.

"I don't envy you the problem." I had long since decided that if it were up to me, the police would have been notified already. Selden may or may not have been an innocent man, but it seems to me that we take too much upon ourselves if we choose to value our own uneducated judgment over the outcome of a legitimate judicial process.

"I am concerned that if the authorities are brought into this without proper preparation, the Lionels may suffer for their action. Although I think their judgment was unsound, I cannot condemn them for their human failings. It is even possible that Selden, having been taken, might implicate them to such an extent that they both might face considerable legal difficulties of their own."

I recognized the possibilities he was suggesting but could think of no way to get around them. Sir Henry, however, had clearly given this considerable thought.

"I have decided to apprehend Mr. Selden myself. I will then instruct him upon the best way to explain his survival in our unwelcoming swamp without implicating his sister and her husband. It would not be to his advantage to ruin them along with himself, and if he's the man his sister believes him to be, he will see the logic of my argument and accept my solution. If on the other hand he is vindictive and uncaring and insists upon dragging them through the mud behind him, I will do my best for them afterwards. In either case, Selden must not be allowed to remain at large."

"Aren't you taking rather a large risk? He is, after all, a likely murderer." I found the entire idea alarming. I was here because Wanda had suggested that Sir Henry might be at risk. She would hardly be pleased to discover that I had allowed him to sally forth on a gallant mission to beard a killer in his lair.

"I will be armed. I am quite a good shot with a revolver."

Heroism is not one of my character traits, but neither is cowardice. "You can't go out there alone. I have a weapon of my own, and the least I can do is provide a second set of eyes and ears."

"I accept your offer, young man. Although I feel obligated to intercede, I'm a bit too old and settled for a life of action." His obvious enthusiasm put the lie to his words.

"How are we to go about it?"

"Selden will be back tonight for more warm food. We know where the rendezvous is set and the approximate time. The biggest difficulty will be slipping out of the house without alerting the Lionels."

I confess that my nerves began to act up when I contemplated what lay before us and I made a point of avoiding the Lionels out of fear that I might inadvertently give away something of our plans. As far as I could see, they were perfectly willing to pretend that our encounter the previous night had never taken place and I presumed they accepted this as tacit acceptance if not actual approval of their course of action. Supper that evening was – or at least seemed – unusually subdued and I retreated to my room right afterward, pretending to have become engrossed in a novel. Sir Henry, as always, retreated to the library and presumably his brandy.

We expected Selden to arrive at around two in the morning but we wanted to be in position long before then. Sir Henry tapped on my door just after midnight. We made our way to the rarely used rear staircase and down to the pantry. After assuring ourselves that no one was in the kitchen, we slipped out the back door. Sir Henry had brought two flashlights, but we didn't dare use them at this point lest we alert someone in the house – or someone watching the house – so it was with some minor difficulty that we made our way around the rear of the Manor and past the garage, then parallel to the tree line until we reached a point where we could observe the head of the trail without being observed ourselves.

And then we waited.

It must have been about ninety minutes and sometimes I think they were the longest ninety minutes of my life. It was somewhat warmer than it had been, but our enforced inactivity allowed the night chill to penetrate our coats and I was shivering slightly when we saw the lights, first from the window of the Manor, and then much closer, right where we expected it to be. A minute or two passed before Mrs. Lionel emerged carrying a wicker basket. She walked straight to the light and there was a faint murmuring which was not loud enough for us to hear clearly. Then she turned and went back toward the Manor, carrying a different basket, and by the manner in which she carried it I could tell that it was considerably lighter than the first.

The light in the window had only lasted a few seconds and the second one disappeared now. Sir Henry stirred himself and I followed suit. The two of us crossed the grass reasonably quietly but with some haste. Selden was no longer there, of course, but I spotted a small patch of light moving through the trees and we set off in pursuit.

We used our own lights but kept them aimed at the ground so that it wasn't likely that Selden would be able to detect our presence. Even though we had walked along this path before, it felt different at night and I took a nasty poke near one eye from a branch that hung in the way, and both of us stumbled on more than one occasion. Fortunately Selden must have had similar difficulties because the gap between us seemed to remain constant, and of course he was buried by the basket he carried.

A quarter hour passed and we were well away from the Manor when a piercing though distant cry echoed through the night. We both stopped where we were, and I saw Selden's light freeze, indicating that he too must have come to a halt.

"What in the world was that?" I asked.

"It sounded like some kind of bird of prey. I imagine there are owls in the swamp." But Sir Henry didn't sound entirely confident. "It's quite far off."

A few seconds later it came again, sharper and more distinct, and very obviously much closer. "One of the local people mentioned having heard something howling in the night." Sir Henry's whispered voice was taut with strain. "I didn't think anything of it at the time. You don't suppose there is any truth to this family curse business, do you?"

"Hippogriffs aren't real," I said, but I doubt very much that I was providing much reassurance. "There is something out there, all right. That wasn't imaginary. And we're outside the suppressive spell by now."

"What if someone used magic to create one? I know it wouldn't be real in a biological sense, but an artificial being could be just as deadly, couldn't it? And if someone had wanted Uncle Charles to die, apparently as the result of our old family curse, that might explain the odd circumstances of his death." For the first time in my experience, he sounded nervous.

I shook my head, but Sir Henry couldn't have seen the gesture in the dark so I spoke aloud. "He died inside the protected area, remember? A homunculus is certainly possible but it would have been unable to pass through the barrier."

"I suppose you're right."

There had been no third occurrence of the sound and ahead of us, Selden's light began to move again. "Do you still want to follow him?" I asked.

"Indeed I do. He may be no more than a distraction, but he's a significant one."

So we resumed our silent, almost slow motion chase. It was taking much longer to cover the ground than it had during the daylight and I had no idea how far we'd come when we suddenly emerged into a cleared area and I realized where we were. The steep descent to the swamps proper was directly ahead of us, and a dark figure was cautiously descending and no longer far ahead of us. In fact, we'd given ourselves away because it stopped and directed the light back in our direction.

Selden knew we were there.

CHAPTER THIRTEEN

Since we knew we had been discovered, we raised our lights and directed them toward our quarry. He, on the other hand, doused his own and vanished from our sight so suddenly that I suspected invisibility charm of some sort, although the intensity of the darkness was probably the real explanation. He was not so successful in masking his sounds, however, and we heard him thrashing his way through the vines and briars that grew in profusion. Selden must have passed this way many times before and he was certainly more familiar with his surroundings than we were and, even with the advantage of light, we fell behind.

If the going had been rough before, it was doubly so now. The ground under our feet was treacherous, not just because of jagged stones but also because patches of what appeared to be solid earth were in fact treacly mud that held our feet so firmly that there was an audible sucking sound when we broke free. We had forgotten to provide ourselves with proper footware for this terrain. No words passed between us, but I for one would have been amenable to abandoning the chase and notifying the police. The possibility of an ambush also occurred to me and I was inclined to move forward less precipitously, compelled to do so only because Sir Henry was clearly determined that Selden should not escape.

My companion had taken the lead and seemed certain that he was heading in the proper direction, but there were no longer any indications that I could see that we were on a distinct trail at all, and for all I knew, Selden was off in some other direction. I was short of breath by now – I felt a tinge of shame that a much older man was clearly in better shape than I – and decided against expressing my doubts just yet.

I won't draw this out. The outcome of our planning and pursuit was complete failure. I had already become convinced that he had evaded us by the time Sir Henry finally came to a sudden halt, breathing heavily and with his shoulders slumped.

"The confounded rascal has given us the slip, I'm afraid. I thought so a while ago but I believed that perhaps if we continued our own blundering way, he might be close by and panic so that we could get our bearings and a fresh trail. But either he is beyond range of our hearing or he is clever enough to remain where he is and allow us to make fools of ourselves. As it is, we might have some difficulty in retracing our path. I apologize for making you a victim of my poor judgment."

"I came willingly and your plan seemed well conceived to me," I said quietly. "It was just bad luck that we failed."

"Well, I think the best thing is to find our way back and in the morning I will reluctantly make a call to the police. I won't involve the Lionels. I'll simply say that we saw someone walking in the swamp and that he took to his heels when he saw us approaching."

We had by this time come to a point so low that even where there were breaks in the tree line, we could not see the lights from the Manor. There were two flanking the front door that were kept illuminated all night and Sir Henry had left one on in the library upstairs. Other than the moonlight, the only lighter patch we could see came from behind a low hill some distance from where we stood. Grimalkin has street lights and I had no doubt that their distant glow was responsible.

I was using this as a reference point to estimate the distance and direction we should have to travel when I saw something move near the crest. At first it seemed just a fleeting shadow, perhaps cast by a wisp of cloud, but then it emerged into the open and I could see that it was a human figure. Naturally my instinct was to believe that Selden had revealed himself, but I immediately doubted that conclusion. Even in that brief glimpse, I had been able to tell that the convict was relatively short but quite heavy in body. The figure I watched now was taller and far more slender. It also wore a peaked hat and I was quite certain that Selden had been bare headed. Could it be some local farmer? Surely it was far too early for even the most industrious to be about.

I was about to call Sir Henry's attention to the figure when it suddenly moved away and vanished from view. I decided not to mention it lest Sir Henry decide it must after all be the fugitive and launch into yet another fruitless pursuit.

So we turned and made our way back to Baskerville Manor.

It was not an easy or pleasant journey, made even more bitter by our complete failure to accomplish anything. It was fortunate that Sir Henry had hunted on the moors back in England because he proved to be at least a moderately good tracker and the two of us had left plenty of evidence of our passing. Even I could pick out some of the footprints pressed deeply into the mud.

We returned to our rooms by the same surreptitious manner in which we'd left them, and I was confident that the Lionels would have no hint of our excursion. Sir Henry reminded me just before we separated that it would be necessary to clean our own shoes in the morning before breakfast and I resigned myself to the chore with as good grace as I could manage.

It started to rain toward morning, the intensity such that it even woke me up at one point despite my immense fatigue. The dim light even at eight was so oppressive that I had to drag myself out of bed and the sense of failure and impending trouble was almost a palpable weight.

By the time breakfast was served – Sir Henry looked fresh as a daisy and I momentarily resented his resilience – it had begun to thunder in earnest. I was resigned to spending the day indoors, but we had pretty much finished going through Charles Baskerville's papers and I wasn't sure just how I would occupy my time unless Sir Henry had something for me to do. I might even be reduced to reading the thriller that I had lately pretended to be engrossed in.

The food revived me somewhat and I followed Sir Henry to the library, planning to finish the last of the filing, but my supposed employer waved me off. "It can wait. You look as though you could do with a nap."

My resentment rose again, but I forced it down. He was certainly correct and his intentions were obviously sincere. So I retired to my room and lay down, but naturally I found myself completely incapable of falling asleep. Instead, the story of the curse and the death of Charles Baskerville kept chasing themselves through my head.

I decided to enumerate just those things which were almost certainly factual. I retrieved my notebook from its hiding place and made a list.

1. The original Baskerville curse was almost certainly authentic. It had been intended to punish those of that family line whose sins were sufficient to merit their death. A number of Baskervilles had succumbed to the curse, which invoked a

hippogriff for their execution. Since the hippogriff is not a natural creation, this had to have been some form of homunculi, an artificial being with as little self awareness as a toaster.

2. Several generations in the past, while the family still resided exclusively in England, steps had been taken to nullify the curse. There had been no further appearances of the hippogriff either there or in America after one branch of the family emigrated.

3. Sir Henry Baskerville was the last representative of the family in England. Charles had been the last of the American line. All other offshoots other than the most remote – the Peters – were extinct.

4. Shortly before the tragic death of Charles Baskerville there had been sightings in the valley of a creature which appeared to be a hippogriff. None of these sightings were within the grounds of Baskerville Manor, which was protected by a nullification spell which would have prevented a magical construct from entering.

5. Charles Baskerville had died, well within the protective barrier. Hoof prints had been found near the body and his face had been clawed by something resembling a raptor's claws. These wounds had not been fatal. The victim had died of heart failure while running across the lawn, presumably in an attempt to escape whatever had attacked him.

6. There was an escaped felon hiding in the swamp. However, Selden had still been imprisoned at the time of Charles' death and could not be responsible. His presence seemed to be unrelated.

7. There was no evidence that Charles had led anything but the most commendable of lives, and therefore even if the family curse had somehow been revived, it is most unlikely that he would have had anything to fear from it.

8. Sir Henry also seemed to be an upright and honorable man, one whom the curse would not affect, but given that his uncle had been killed, it seemed plausible that he might also be a prospective victim. He had, however, concealed the fact that he was acquainted with an unidentified woman whom he had met with in Grimalkin.

Based on all of this, I concluded that there was a strong possibility that Sir Henry was also at risk, although I could not for the life of me think of a motive for anyone of whom I was aware. I wondered briefly about the Peters family, who seemed to be the only people with an interest in Sir Henry's death. I also decided that the family curse could not have been responsible for the attack on Charles Baskerville, despite appearances. Even if he led some secret life of intense evil, he could not have been struck down magically unless he'd ventured outside the barrier.

Which meant there had to have been a human agency involved. But I had no idea who that person might be, or what possible motive they might have possessed. And I still didn't know the identity of the mysterious man whom we had encountered back in Boston. I was reasonably certain now that it had not been Lionel, although I could not absolutely rule him out. I had met only a handful of the local inhabitants, so it might be one of the farmers, but even if I were introduced to the man I might not recognize him. The beard might have been false or his appearance altered through a charm of disguise. It's unlikely that he could conceal his general build because that sort of charm tended to break up when the subject moved quickly within a crowd, but his face could have been transformed almost completely.

It felt better to have the outline down in print, but I lost much of my enthusiasm when I realized that I could not construct a single reasonable hypothesis based on those facts. The only straw I could take hold of was the question of Sir Henry's estate. I decided that it was advisable to look into the whereabouts of the various members of the Peters family, particularly if any of them had recently visited America.

I had spent more than an hour on these ruminations and none of that time actually sleeping, but I did feel somewhat refreshed. I returned to the library where I found Sir Henry going through the day's mail, separating bills from circulars.

"You've remembered about the shoes, I hope."

I nodded. "I'm afraid they'll never be quite the same again. I packed them in my bag for safe keeping. Fortunately I brought another pair."

He tossed a small pile of correspondence into the trash basket. "I may actually have some work for you this afternoon. I've decided to liquidate some of my interests back in England and reinvest the money here where I can watch it more closely."

"Have you decided to make your residence here permanently then?"

"Let us say, rather, than my time here will be extended indefinitely. I feel comfortable in the Manor, but once the Lionels are gone and I have to find suitable replacements, I might discover that it is not as congenial as I'd hoped. And I have yet to meet most of my tenants."

I remembered his reported encounter with a woman in Grimalkin but decided it would be inappropriate for me to mention it unless he raised the subject.

"I've called the police as planned." He frowned. "They didn't seem particularly excited by the news. I think they believed I might have seen some perfectly innocent person and allowed my imagination to run away with me."

"You can only do what lies within your grasp, Sir Henry. If they don't act on your information, the fault doesn't lie with you."

"No, I suppose not."

I fidgeted. "I wanted to ask you something, but it might be impertinent, so feel free to ignore me."

"My dear man, after last night's mutual excursion, I feel that we have become friends of a sort. Ask what you will."

"I was just wondering what would happen to the Baskerville estate if something were to happen to you? I mean, with your uncle dead, you're the last of the family. You mentioned a distant cousin, I believe. Would he stand to inherit both the Hall and the Manor?"

"In the absence of a will, I believe that would be the case. Don't think that the question has not occurred to me as well. I have been making some notes and have already asked Mortimer to recommend a good lawyer. I feel no great affection for my cousin, you understand, but he is the closest I have to family and it is only right that the Hall should go to him, along with the associated properties and investments. The Manor and the bulk of my portfolio I propose to leave to another party, but there are certain conditions that must be met before I can write a formal will."

"You might want to expedite that process. If the motive behind your uncle's murder was material gain, then you are clearly the last remaining obstacle. I don't mean to impugn your cousin," I added hastily. "But there is clearly some malign intelligence at work here."

"I agree completely. In fact, I have employed a private investigator in Wales to ascertain whether or not my cousin and/or his two sons have been away from home for any extended period of time recently, particularly whether or not they have visited America. I expect a report from them any day now."

"They could, however, have hired the services of another party."

"Quite true. But I'm not my uncle and it's unlikely they will be able to frighten me to death. And in any case, I hope within a few days to have met with one of your local lawyers and made over the bulk of my estate to my wife."

"Your wife?" I must have looked as dumbfounded as I felt because he chuckled.

"No, I haven't lied to you or Miss Coyne. I am still a bachelor, although I hope to remedy that condition quite soon. I have fallen in love, you see, and am ready to ask that most important of questions. And once I have my answer, if it's the answer I desire, then the will shall be made. For the present time, I must keep my own council. If the lady should refuse me, I would not care to have the details known, even to those sympathetic to my cause."

"But your cousin still stands to inherit a substantial legacy," I pointed out.

At this he laughed heartily. "And good luck to him with it. The property is so encumbered that it barely generates any income and the land is not so desirable that it could be sold off profitably. If he lives as simple a life as I was forced to do, he will be able to maintain the property by means of the rents he receives, but he will hardly be able to lead a life of leisure."

He leaned forward. "I, on the other hand, plan to do exactly that. I will attempt to emulate my uncle in almost every way save that I will have a wife to keep me company. And curse or not, I plan to enjoy that life for a very long time."

CHAPTER FOURTEEN

I dreamt that night of the figure I'd seen in the swamps. In my dream, I pursued him through a nightmare landscape that reached up with sticky hands to paw at my legs as I passed. Ahead of me, the unknown other moved with effortless grace, unhampered by the terrain. I sensed that this was not a stranger that I followed and sometimes I was sure it was the mystery man from Boston and sometimes I was equally convinced that it was Lionel. Of course, it was not impossible for it to be both. But there were still other times when I was sure that it was someone else entirely, someone I knew but whose identity eluded me.

I woke early and lay in bed, gathering the last tenuous strings of my dream memories together. Was there some actual insight to be drawn from the playfulness of my subconscious? Could Lionel have left the Manor and reached the point where I'd seen the stranger? It seemed entirely plausible although I could not for the life of me imagine any reason why he would indulge in any such activity. And certainly the bearded man could have traveled to the valley at any time. He might be a resident. He might be an outsider. There were rooms he could have taken both north and south of the valley and with an automobile, he would be less than an hour away. But wouldn't someone notice if a stranger drove into the valley late at night? Transient traffic after dark was almost nonexistent.

Sir Henry was uncharacteristically preoccupied at breakfast that morning. Although he had seemed unaffected at first by our fruitless quest into the swamps, perhaps his reaction had only been delayed. He seemed to hold himself tautly, as though he was apprehensive about some immediate physical danger to himself. He did take the car out early in the afternoon, but when I proposed joining him he politely but firmly told me that he needed some personal time. I wondered if he was planning another clandestine meeting with the woman he was courting – as clandestine as was possible in a community as small as Grimalkin – and that cheered me for a while, at least until I considered the possibility that his romantic interest might be connected to the conspiracy against the Baskerville family interests. If the marriage took place, she would be the immediate beneficiary of Sir Henry's death.

I should also mention that there is now tension between Sir
Henry and the Lionels. A detective from the state police stopped by
to talk to Sir Henry and I about our sighting of an unknown man in
the swamps. We had put together a more plausible explanation of
that event which made no reference to the Lionels, but they were of
course aware that we must have approached the authorities. Neither
of them expressed their displeasure verbally but our supper that night
had been somewhat overcooked and heavily salted, and Lionel was
stiff and took his time answering when he was summoned. I was
sure Sir Henry had noticed this insolence, but apparently he chose
not to make an issue of it and it was certainly not my place to do so.
The irony of this is that the detective was clearly convinced that we
had been mistaken and that our imaginations had run away with us.

While Sir Henry was out, I finished the novel I had been reading
– the ending was contrived and predictable – and found myself with
nothing to do. It had started to rain again, a fine drizzle that was
miserable without being exciting, so it was impossible to go for a
walk. After rearranging my clothing unnecessarily, I wandered to the
library to see if there was any filing that I had left incomplete,
although I knew full well that every document was in its assigned
place.

I was sitting at the heavy oak desk when pure chance took a
hand. I had cracked open one of the windows to allow some
circulation – the library had a faintly musty smell – when a sudden
gust of wind rattled the window and made me jump. My elbow hit
Sir Henry's fountain pen, which rolled across the desktop and –
before I could catch hold of it – tumbled down between the desk and
the wall.

The desk was a monstrously heavy piece of furniture and there
was no possible way that I could shift it unassisted to retrieve the
pen. Nor was there enough room between desk and wall for me to
reach in far enough to catch hold of it that way. I fretted for a few
seconds, then went to my room and took a wire coat hanger from the
closet. After a few minutes of probing, I had drawn out of hiding the
wayward pen, a pair of paper clips, and a small sheet of writing
paper.

The paper was a note addressed to Charles Baskerville and it was
written in a woman's hand. It asked him to meet with the writer that
night at precisely eight o'clock. There was a sketch at the bottom

showing the Manor and the stone wall, with an "X" at end of the wall. The date was as familiar one, for it was the very same day that Charles Baskerville had died. Lionel had found his body shortly before nine. The note was signed only by initials – L.L.

I knew with absolute certainty that this was an important clue, and wished that I had found it by reasoning rather than happenstance. It was significant enough that I even went to the den and tried to reach Wanda by telephone, but there was no answer. I chafed at the necessity of remaining patient and wondered whether or not I should tell Sir Henry of my discovery.

I returned to the library and opened the file drawer where the leases were kept. Four of the tenants had last names that began with the letter "L", but only one of the men had the double initial, Lawrence Linney, and none of the wives. There might be a daughter or other relation whose name would fit, but they would not have been mentioned in the rental documents. It was also possible that someone in Grimalkin who did not actually lease their property from the Baskerville estate might be L.L., but I had no way of determining if that was the case. I recalled the bartender, Liz, and went downstairs to find Lionel.

My pretext for mentioning the bar seemed quite artificial to me, but Lionel seemed to take it in stride. He admitted that he stopped there from time to time. "It's a bit loud at times but the owner keeps things under control. Younger people don't have many places to entertain themselves in the valley, sir. It serves a useful purpose."

"Who is the owner? I met the bartender, Liz something or another, when I stopped by but no one else seemed to be around."

"That would be Elizabeth Lawrence, sir. She has been the owner since her father died a few years ago."

The odds favored her being the writer of the note. But why would Charles Baskerville be meeting clandestinely with Liz Lawrence, I wondered. He was old enough to be her father.

Sir Henry returned after a couple of hours and he brought the mail with him. There was an envelope for me, and I was cheered to see that it was postmarked from Boston. Inside was a brief typed note from Wanda apologizing for her long silence. "I have nearly cleared up this other matter and hope to join you within a few days." It was the best news I had heard since arriving in the valley.

Having announced that he was suffering from an intense headache, Sir Henry took himself off to his bedroom for a nap. I decided that there was no urgent reason why he should know about the note I had found, and I had thought of a way to refine what little I already knew about it.

Lionel didn't blink when I told him I was taking the car. The drizzle had become intermittent but it was heavily overcast and when I glanced toward the swamp, I could see that a thick haze or fog clung to it like a blanket. Selden might be a criminal, even a killer, but it was difficult not to feel some sympathy for him, living like an animal out in that unpleasantness.

I drove directly to the village and parked as before in front of the clinic. James was in, was in fact just saying goodbye to a patient – a dark haired woman whose little boy had his arm in a sling – when I entered the building. He greeted me heartily as they left and asked how things were at the Manor. "I've been meaning to stop by but there's been a rash of minor ailments lately."

After assuring him that all was well, I told him that we had found a couple of documents referring to someone with the initials L.L. but had been unable to identify this individual by their full name and wondered if he could help. I did not mention the note itself or its contents.

He frowned in concentration. "There's Lucy Linney, but she's only three years old. And Lester Long, but he died of cancer. Those are the only names I can think of offhand. Is it important?"

"I don't know. The notes suggest that Charles might have owed this person some money, but there's nothing definitive. Might it have been Liz Lawrence?"

"Lizzie? Never thought of her. Elizabeth's her legal name, of course. I can't imagine Charles owing her money unless he kept a bar tab, and Charles was never really much of a drinker. He stopped in from time to time to be sociable but he was never really part of that crowd. They tended to be a lot younger."

"Could they have had some kind of business arrangement?"

James shrugged. "I suppose it's possible, but I can't imagine what it could have been. Lizzie owns the bar free and clear and it makes money, though not very much. No real competition within twenty miles. She wouldn't have needed a partner."

"Maybe she was planning to expand?"

"I doubt it. She has trouble filling the place as it is. Why don't you just ask her? She's probably behind the bar right now."

I felt an odd reluctance to beard the woman in her own lair, so to speak, but I thought my cover story might hold up. I thanked James and took my leave, walking the short distance to the Black Goat Tavern.

It was considerably more crowded this time and most of the places at the bar were filled, along with all of the booths and tables. I realized then that this was Saturday. Time had a way of blending one day into the next in the valley and I hadn't realized that it was already the weekend. Most of the people were about my own age, late twenties and early thirties, although there were a few older faces scattered throughout the crowd. Liz was behind the bar, assisted by a young man I'd never seen before. I had to admire the efficient way in which she filled requests and I moved to a vantage point where I could watch for a while. No money seemed to be changing hands and I never saw Liz or her assistant record a sale, but I had no doubt that tabs were being run and that accurate tallies would be proffered and paid without question. There was an atmosphere of trust in that bar that I had never encountered in Boston, or anywhere else for that matter. Small town life was not without its compensations.

The press of people was daunting. I did manage to order a drink but it was quite clear that I was not going to have an opportunity to talk to her until the activity died down. I nursed my beer – and later a second - in solitude and watched the ebb and flow for over an hour before I realized that there was not going to be a let-up for a long time to come. I was not patient enough to wait around until closing time some four hours off, so I managed to pay my tab – the young man correctly interpreted my expression and gave me the total – along with a generous tip.

On the way back to the Manor, I mused that Wanda would undoubtedly have found a way to arrange an interview despite the crowd. I had a perhaps somewhat exaggerated opinion of her capacity to solve problems. The two beers had left me somewhat lightheaded – I had had a light lunch and as yet no supper – so I drove with exaggerated care.

My hyper alertness did have an interesting result, however. As I was passing through the large gate, I saw movement within the line of trees to my left. The turn from the main road is somewhat acute when coming from the village and I had decelerated sharply. My attention was divided between maneuvering the car and following that sudden movement, so I can't be certain that I interpreted the shape correctly, but I was quite convinced that the figure of a man had retreated into the darkness when my headlights had turned in that direction.

CHAPTER FIFTEEN

I was in a foul mood when I reached the Manor and as it happened, Lionel opened the door for me and took the brunt of my irritation. The fact that I was certainly justified does not excuse my manners, which were brusque and antagonistic. I asked him to join me in the den for a moment, but my tone made it clear that it was not a request.

As soon as we reached that room, I rounded on him. "I find it difficult to understand why you continue to put your employer into such a difficult position."

Lionel was an intelligent man. He surmised correctly and immediately that I was talking about Selden. "We have tried to do our best in a difficult situation. My wife is very fond of her brother despite his less than exemplary life, and I am very fond of my wife."

"Your loyalty to your wife notwithstanding, you must see that the situation is intolerable. Sir Henry is indirectly helping a fugitive from the law, a convicted murderer no less, and knowingly doing so."

Lionel looked uncomfortable. "We had hoped to conceal our activities from him. Once he learned the truth, we told Selden that we could not help him any further and that he would have to leave the valley immediately. Sir Henry is no longer complicit in his evasion of the authorities in any way."

"Are you telling me that you sent him away?"

"Oh, yes. We provided one final parcel of food and some other necessities and he promised that he would be out of the valley within twenty-four hours. I didn't ask where he intended to go and he didn't volunteer the information. Neither my wife nor I can be of any conceivable help to the police."

"But I saw him in the woods just a few minutes ago," I protested.

For the first time I saw the butler's face dissolve into confusion. "I don't understand how that is possible. He was most sincere in his promise to quit the area immediately. In fact he'd been planning to do so within a day or two in any case. The hue and cry has died down now and he has grown enough of a beard that he no longer resembles the pictures that have been published. We provided him with some clothing that will not arouse suspicion. He has also lost some weight. Once he puts some distance between himself and the valley, I believe he will have no trouble blending in. He possesses considerable natural cunning."

I tried to remember what the figure in the trees had looked like, but he'd only been visible for a second. I was about to offer some awkward form of apology when he surprised me. "It may have been the other man."

"What other man?" Of course, I already had a pretty good idea what he was talking about.

"There's been a second man living in the swamps. Selden caught sight of him once or twice and one night noticed sparks rising from his fire. He was careful to stay clear, of course, and remained on his guard afterward. The other man kept to himself, but on one occasion Selden saw him from a distance. He was coming from the direction of the village and was carrying a large knapsack."

I remembered the small grocery in Grimalkin. "Provisions, do you think?"

"I'm sure I wouldn't know, but that would be the logical conclusion."

"Then someone might remember him."

"I can't speak to that, but some of the farmers hire seasonal help during planting season. There are a number of strangers here now, although most of them are regulars. And the residents have guests from time to time, not to mention people driving through who stop to shop. There is a state park just south of the valley and they have a popular camping area. Grimalkin is the closest grocery."

"But a man with a knapsack?"

Lionel shrugged. "As to that, I couldn't say. But we also have our share of hikers."

I was thoughtful for a moment and Lionel made as if to leave. "One last question. Did Selden say where this other man made his camp?"

"After a fashion. He mentioned that it was up near the old burial grounds. At least that's where he saw the fire."

"All right. Thank you for your candor. And I wouldn't mention this to Sir Henry if I were you. At least not unless he asks you directly."

"I would not wish to add to his troubles unnecessarily."

I had not yet confided in Sir Henry about my suspicions regarding Liz Lawrence. I decided to withhold this latest intelligence as well, at least for the moment. I now suspected that the man I had just seen in the woods was also the figure I'd watched disappear into the cemetery. And both of them were undoubtedly the person I'd spotted in the distance while Sir Henry and I were engaged in our unsuccessful hunt for Selden. It was entirely possible that this was just some vagrant or eccentric, although if so he showed a recurring interest in Baskerville Manor. Could it be that this interest was malevolent? Could he be the force behind the rumors of a hippogriff and the death of Charles Baskerville? And if so, was he even now planning a similar fate for Sir Henry?

I desperately wished that I could speak to Wanda. My experience in situations like this was very limited and she always seemed to know precisely what course of action was most likely to have satisfactory results. I was floundering. Should I tell all to Sir Henry and put him on his guard, or would I be worrying him for no good reason?

I was still wrestling with this problem the following morning when fate took a hand. Sir Henry had announced his intention of lunching in the village and it was quite evident that he desired no company, or at least not mine. It was obvious that he was having another assignation with the woman he intended to marry. I could think of no good reason why he would not have invited her to the Manor – we certainly provided enough chaperoning to satisfy any European standard of propriety – but it was not my place to question him, even though I fretted when he left the Manor alone.

He had complained of a headache and restless stomach at breakfast, which I had assumed was precipitated by his fondness for brandy. I would not say that I had ever seen Sir Henry actually drunk but he certainly consumed more than was good for him. About mid-morning he announced that he was going for a walk to clear his head and I invited myself along, ignoring his gentle hints that he wanted to be alone.

At first we conversed inconsequentially. It was quite warm that morning and Sir Henry was wearing a vest and jacket. I could see the beads of sweat on his forehead and I thought his breathing was a bit labored. Sensing that he no longer wished to talk, I fell into a silence and was in fact quite caught up in my own thoughts when I realized that he was in distress.

Tact will draw a curtain over the next few moments. Suffice it to say that Sir Henry rather violently expelled his breakfast and was quite pale when he allowed me to lead him back to the house. Mrs. Lionel was told to brew some strong tea and Sir Henry went up to his bedroom. Half an hour later, Lionel informed me that I was wanted.

Sir Henry was in bed and he looked to be quite miserable. He was still sweating profusely and his face looked puffy and off color. His voice was hoarse and weak. "Everdeen, I need to ask a favor."

"I'm at your service."

"I have an appointment in town today, at the Black Goat Tavern. It's too late to call and put it off – she's already on her way by now – and I'm obviously in no condition to go. Could I ask you to meet her in my stead and explain that I was suddenly taken ill?"

I had to struggle to keep from showing just how willing I was. At last I was to meet the woman Sir Henry hoped to make his wife. "I'd be happy to help."

"Her name is Lydia Longtree. She'll be alone in one of the booths. I don't have a picture but she's a handsome woman about my own age. Dresses well. Wears glasses. I don't imagine you'll have any trouble picking her out, particularly at this time of the day."

The tavern would be empty and I had no doubt that he was right, but my mind was running full speed now. I had assumed that L.L. was Liz Lawrence, but here was another candidate.

Sir Henry reached to his night table and picked up a handful of currency which he proffered to me. "Have lunch with her and convey my apologies. Tell her that I'll be in touch tomorrow and that I deeply regret having missed her."

I accepted the money and tucked it into my pocket. "What should I say if she decides to visit your sickbed?"

He shook his head. "That question won't arise. We have agreed that she should not visit the Manor until we are ready to make a formal announcement. Among other things, I would not want her to take the risk. Although it does appear that whatever danger hovered over my uncle may no longer exist."

I remembered our mysterious lurker but I didn't say anything. Sir Henry had hoped to the last for a miraculous recovery so I was forced to leave promptly. Questions chased themselves through my mind as I drove to Grimalkin.

As predicted, I had no difficulty identifying Miss Longtree. Other than Liz, she was the only female in the tavern, and almost the only customer. Two men sat in another booth and a third was hunched over a beer at the bar.

"Miss Longtree?" She looked up at me and I was immediately struck by how attractive she was. I would have put her age as nearing forty but she was clearly an active, healthy woman. I quickly introduced myself and explained my presence. Her expression was as much amused as disappointed as she invited me to join her.

"You're the secretary, aren't you?"

"Yes," I admitted. "It's only temporary. Once we have the estate papers organized, I will be returning to Boston." The papers were in fact well in hand, thanks to Charles Baskerville's careful management, but I wasn't ready to admit that. "It has been quite a pleasant posting. The Manor is very comfortable."

"Yes, I recall it being so."

I couldn't avoid looking surprised. "I understood that you hadn't visited it yet."

"Not since Henry has been here, but I was there socially on a few occasions while Charles was still alive."

"You knew him then?"

"Yes." She didn't elaborate. I fancy that I am quite good at evaluating people – Wanda frequently asks my opinion of new clients – and I had already decided that there was something more to Lydia Longtree than was obvious. There was steel there, hidden below the surface. Cold steel.

"And how did you meet Sir Henry, if you don't mind my asking?"

"It's not a secret. I decided to spend a few months in England this year and Charles told me that I should look up his nephew. I did so and we became quite friendly. At the time we even talked about his paying a visit to the States so that I could return his hospitality. Of course we had no reason to suspect how quickly that trip would come or why it would be necessary."

"Were you there when he received the news?"

"No, I'd left a couple of weeks earlier."

Liz came over and took our orders. The tavern did mostly sandwiches and salads, but they sounded appetizing.

"You don't live in the valley?"

"Not any longer. My late father was one of the tenants, but he had no sons and left me rather badly off when he died. Charles Baskerville helped me set up a little business of my own in Celador, a small town up north. I left the valley more than a decade ago."

"What kind of business?"

"It's a crafts and gift shop. The income isn't spectacular but it's steady and adequate and I enjoy the work."

"Was Charles actively involved?" She gave me a sharp look. "I ask because there's no mention of it in the paperwork we've examined. If he holds an interest in your business, then we need to account for it."

"It was a private loan and I paid it off some time ago. He gave me the promissory note when I made the final payment and I burned it. There is no longer any financial relationship between myself and the Baskerville family."

"When was the last time you saw Charles?"

There was a sudden glint in her eyes. "Why do you ask?"

"Sir Henry and I have been discussing the circumstances of his uncle's death. It seems quite mysterious. I wondered if he had told anyone that he was in fear of his life, or dropped any other hint that something might be wrong. So long as the mystery is unsolved, the possibility of danger hangs over Sir Henry as well. I feel a degree of loyalty to my employer, who has been most kind."

"Sir Henry strikes me as quite capable of protecting himself."

"That might well be, but he also would like closure on his uncle's death."

She considered that for a while. "The answer to your question is that I had not met with Charles Baskerville at all during the last several months of his life. Our business was concluded when I paid back his loan, and we had little else in common. I appreciated the assistance he provided when I needed it, but we were not in any sense close friends."

Our food came and we ate without speaking for several minutes. I think both of us had become suspicious by now. Longtree undoubtedly considered my questions as bordering upon the impertinent. For my part, I was convinced that she was concealing something or perhaps lying outright. I decided that I could not injure the relationship between the two of us any further by being blunt, so I sallied forth.

"You said that you hadn't seen Charles Baskerville for several months prior to his death. Did you perhaps carry on any correspondence with him during that period?"

"Not that I recall. There was no further business between us."

"Then you didn't arrange to see him on the day that he died? We found a note among his papers to that effect."

I faced open hostility now and wondered if I had gone too far. "Are you calling me a liar?"

"Of course not." But I was. "It may have slipped your memory but I assure you the note still exists."

"Then it is a forgery. What did it say exactly?"

"It requested that Charles meet you that evening at a remote spot near the Manor."

"I told you, I haven't been to the Manor in more than a year."

"Not inside, perhaps. But you might have been on the grounds."

She sat back and regarded me with open dislike. "And how do you know that this note came from me? Was it signed?"

"Only with your initials," I admitted.

She laughed, but unpleasantly. "I'm not the only person with those initials. Have you talked to Leonard Lymington? They were partners in some sort of development scheme in New Hampshire. And Liz over there," she gestured toward the bar, "almost lost this place once that I know of and Charles helped her out. There must be others."

I had seen Lymington's name in the estate papers. He had bought out Charles' share almost two years past. And I was quite sure that the note was written in a woman's hand, although I suppose it might have been forged.

The rest of the meal passed in frosty silence. Longtree declined the offer of dessert and took her leave. I waved my empty coffee cup toward Liz, wanting to sit and think for a bit before proceeding further. She brought over the pot and what I thought was an unnecessary clean cup, but she slid into the booth opposite me and poured for both of us.

"I think you upset the lady."

120

In the nearly empty room, much of what we had said must have been audible. "Sorry if we made a scene."

"Oh, we're used to loud conversations in here. But if you want to keep the Baskerville family's business private, you might want to lower your voice next time."

"You're right, of course. But I am rather fond of Sir Henry and I would really like to get to the bottom of his uncle's death. While it remains unsolved, there is a palpable shadow of danger hanging over his head."

"You said something about a note that Charles received on the day of his death."

"Yes. I thought it might have come from Miss Longtree. It was arranging a meeting about the time of his death."

Liz sipped her coffee and regarded me so openly that I felt a bit uneasy. "Are you a detective of some sort?"

That was a bit close to the mark but I parried. "Amateur only. I'm really a secretary. I work out of Boston and this assignment is just a temporary thing. There are just so many questions…" I let my voice trail off.

"Well, I can answer one of them for you. I'm the one who wrote to Charles Baskerville. I even told the police about it, although they never found the note itself."

"Then you saw him shortly before his death?"

She shook her head. "Nope. I never got there. Have you ever made a really bad decision in your life?"

"I suppose I've made a few."

"No, I mean something so bad that it hovers over your thoughts almost all the time."

I shook my head. "I'm reasonably content with my life, actually. I'm happily married, gainfully employed, in good health and with good prospects."

"I almost married. His name was Randolph Doyle. Does that name mean anything to you?"

"I can't say that it does."

"Well, it would if you lived in Vermont. He's probably the most talented thaumaturgist in the state. Sits on the Board of Governors for the state university, used to serve in the legislature and still has a lot of influence there. He was the Vermont Attorney General a few years back."

I shook my head. "Sorry. I have trouble enough with Boston politics."

"Well, Randolph – he's never Randy – is a few years older than me and strikingly good looking. His sister is married to one of the Baskerville tenants and she introduced me once when he came to visit. Randolph is an impressive guy – handsome, enthusiastic, the kind of person who really makes you feel welcome. I'm surprised he hasn't run for governor by now. Anyway, we hit it off and the next thing I knew we were a couple, except only when he could spare the time to come to the valley. He never married so I was kind of surprised that he wanted to keep things secret. But I was busy with this place and I'm pretty much a country girl, so I didn't really mind that I only shared one part of his life."

I didn't need precognition to see what was coming next.

"But one day I decided to surprise Randolph on his birthday. I knew where he lived, naturally, even though I'd never been there. So I blew my budget and bought a fancy new outfit, ordered an expensive cake and some even more expensive wine, and drove up to the big city to surprise my man. Well, it was a surprise all right. I walked into the middle of a very private party he has having with my city girl counterpart."

"You hadn't suspected that all along?"

She shook her head. "Never. I guess I'm just a naïve country girl. When he told me I was the love of his life, I believed him. It was quite a shock – for both of us as it turned out. I made a scene. I don't remember everything I said but it was pretty melodramatic. She heard most of it, of course, and apparently she didn't know about me either. The servants got an earful, and so did the neighbors when it spilled out of the house. And Randolph was not pleased with me at all."

She lapsed into silence, drank some coffee, and I decided to prompt her. "How did that lead to you writing to Charles Baskerville?"

"Randolph is a powerful man, and a vindictive one. He leaned on someone and questions were raised about my liquor license. I knew where it was coming from but he's used to getting his way and I thought I needed a balancing power. Charles was a good man. I knew I could tell him my story and that he would do his best to make it all go away."

"But why not just go to the Manor itself? Why meet clandestinely outdoors?"

"Because I didn't want the Lionels to know my business. They were fiercely devoted to Charles and I know they eavesdropped whenever they could in order to better protect him. No matter how pure their motives, though, they're busybodies and I didn't want the story about my humiliation to spread here in the valley. I can't stand having people feel sorry for me."

"And did you meet him that day?"

"No, I didn't. I never kept that appointment. I had just started out – I was going to park on the main road and walk up - when Mrs. Ardmore came out of nowhere and ran right in front of me. I didn't hit her hard but it was enough to knock her over. Mortimer James said she should have x-rays and an ethereal cardiogram just to be on the safe side, so we bundled her into my car and the three of us drove down to the emergency room in Moran. Everything checked out but by the time we got back it was hours later. I called the Manor but Lionel told me that Charles had gone for a walk and I decided to apologize and explain in the morning and went to bed. I never saw him again."

CHAPTER SIXTEEN

I paid the check and left soon afterward. My dislike for Lydia Longtree was instinctive. I had no idea what her financial situation might be – she dressed expensively and obviously wasn't struggling to make a living – but she struck me as an adventuress. Sir Henry seemed quite naïve and there had apparently been no previous romantic entanglements, so he was vulnerable prey. But it was none of my business. I was here to help determine whether or not he was in danger from the same agency that had brought about the death of his uncle. I was neither his friend, his clergyman, nor his counselor. And it did not appear that there was anything linking her to his uncle's death.

Liz might have lied to me about what happened the night when Charles Baskerville died, but it could be easily checked and I didn't think she was stupid enough to take such an enormous risk. The tenuous strands which I had chosen to investigate all seemed untethered to anything substantive.

But I was to have a more productive encounter before I left the village. Unlikely as it sounds, my unexpected informant was Mrs. Ardmore. She was sitting on a bench in a small sliver of grass that was what passed for a park in Grimalkin and I had to pass by on my way to where I had parked. She was hunched forward slightly and I thought she was knitting but when I paused to say good day to her, she raised her head and I saw that she was manipulating some sort of talisman.

"You're not the one," she said firmly.

"I beg your pardon?"

"I may be old and losing my wits, but you can't fool me. You're not him."

I might normally have agreed with her and moved along rather than engage in what seemed likely to be a pointless conversation, but there was something about the intensity of her expression that glued me to the spot.

"Who are you looking for?" I asked.

"I'm not as dimwitted as they say, you know. I listen to the radio. I know there's a convict out in the swamps."

I attempted to reassure her that there was no danger. "If he was there before, he is surely gone now. The police believe that he is far away from the valley or they would have caught him."

"No, he's still here. I would know if he'd gone. I can still feel him up here," she tapped the side of her head. "He's gone, but he's still here."

This made absolutely no sense to me and I took a step away, intending to leave. But she arrested me with her next words. "He's not the one I'm watching for."

"Well, who is it then?" I'm afraid I sounded a bit impatient at this point.

"There's no need to snap at me, young man. I'm telling you, aren't I?"

I apologized, but with limited sincerity.

"Someone has to be bringing him food. They haven't thought about that, have they?"

Now I couldn't leave. If Mrs. Ardmore had somehow learned of the Lionels' involvement, it could go badly for them. I knew that the old woman had been deprived of her fey powers, but I also knew that the procedures involved sometimes left shadows of former talents in place. "He could have stolen food from the farms. If he was careful, it wouldn't have been noticed."

She shook her head. "Someone's been helping him. I see their shadows inside my head, but not their faces. There's the one who is hunted and the one who carries food into the swamps."

"What does this other one look like?"

Mrs. Ardmore seemed to have forgotten that I was there, but she responded to the question anyway. "I can't see a face. There is too much shadow and my inner eye is half closed now. But I see it here in the village, at the market, and I see it walking with a heavy pack on its back. It goes out into the swamps. And then I see the hunted one and he has food to eat and even beer to drink and I know that someone is helping him. I have never seen them together, but it must be so."

"But you've never seen a face?"

"Not yet. But I'll recognize the shape when I see it in the flesh and then I'll know the face and I'll tell them the truth. They think I'm a useless old woman, but I still have my uses." And she laughed and went back to her talisman, turning it over and over in her hands.

I wasn't sure how to interpret this. I was reassured that there was no sign that she suspected that the Lionels were involved. But I remembered their report that Selden had seen another figure in the swamps, someone carrying a knapsack, and I suspected this might also be the figure in the peaked hat I had spotted from a distance. Mrs. Ardmore seemed to have had genuine visions, if that's what they were, although they were too indistinct to be particularly useful. But what had she meant when she'd said that Selden was gone but that he was still here in the valley? Was it just some further confusion in her weakened mind or did it have some significance that eluded me?

I was so caught up in my own thoughts that I walked right past the parked car and recovered myself only when I was hailed by a voice I did not at first recognize. It was Frank Lafter, whom I had met when he visited the Manor, and he was walking briskly toward me.

I confess that I was mildly irritated. At that moment, I wanted to thresh out the implications of what Mrs. Ardmore had said. But I couldn't very well pretend that I hadn't heard or seen him so I waited until he reached me and pumped my hand.

"How are things going up at the Manor? A lot of the local people are getting a bit anxious because Sir Henry has been rather reclusive."

"There was a great deal of paperwork to deal with, and he is ill today."

Lafter looked genuinely concerned. "Nothing serious, I hope."

"I don't think so. Too much rich food, I suspect. Mrs. Lionel lays a fancy table."

"That she does. Charles had few vices but eating well was one of them. I understand that the two of you spotted our fugitive the other day."

Obviously I needed to be circumspect. "We may have done so. The police seem to think we just happened on one of the locals out for a walk, or a hiker passing through. They're still of the opinion that the convict has left the vicinity."

"I'm not so sure of that. I've been after them myself, but they are rather stubborn, I'll grant you."

"Have you any new evidence that he's still in the area?"

Lafter looked smug. "Well, I told you about my telescope, didn't I? The day we were out at the Manor, I mean."

I confirmed that he had.

"Last night was particularly clear and I thought I'd take another look at the swamp. I had pretty well accepted that this was a lost cause, but last night I got lucky. I saw something – a pinprick of light – and the shape of a man moved back and forth in front of it for a while before it gradually died away. I am convinced that it was a campfire and that someone was tending it."

Although I was interested, I didn't want to encourage Lafter's enthusiasm. "It might have been some hikers camping out for the night."

"Exactly what Detective Raines said when I called him. He implied that Selden was too smart to start a fire where it could be seen, however unlikely that might be, and that in any case they had reports of his being sighted in the woods way up north of the valley."

The Lionels had not known, or at least had not volunteered to tell us, in which direction Selden might travel. But if he was well away, what did Mrs. Ardmore's strange vision mean, if anything? "Whereabouts was this fire, if that's what it was?"

"Just beyond the burial ground as near as I could tell. It's hard to judge distances under those conditions and there are no real landmarks."

"Isn't that supposed to be dangerous terrain? Why would Selden camp there?"

"For that very reason. Everyone else would avoid the area. Even the police give it a wide berth."

"Are you planning to investigate further?"

"Me? I'm no woodsman. I mentioned it to a couple of the farmers and they just shrugged like it was no business of theirs. I think the burial ground has them spooked as well. I was hoping that you might mention this to Sir Henry. He might have enough influence to force the authorities to actually go out and see for themselves."

"I'm afraid Sir Henry has yet to develop that kind of network. His position brings a degree of respect, of course, but after seeing how easily his own report was dismissed, I think it unlikely that he'd advocate for yours without a more substantial basis, and even if he did, there's not a strong probability that it would result in the kind of action you desire."

Lafter was plainly disappointed, but after a few seconds he nodded. "I suppose that you're right. It's damnably frustrating though. Someone is out there and that someone is trying to avoid being noticed. I'm sure of that as well."

I returned to the Manor to find that Sir Henry was asleep but his color and breathing had improved dramatically. This was good news for more than one reason, for I had hit upon a plan – admittedly in retrospect a somewhat foolish one – and I wanted to place it in motion at the earliest possible opportunity.

First I went to my room and secured my pistol. Then I changed into a pair of calf high boots which I had purchased just in case we needed to wander around in the swamps a second time. Finally I went to the library and found one of the maps of the valley which Charles Baskerville had neatly filed with some handwritten notes of his own sprinkled across its surface. I glanced at this briefly, then rolled it up and took it with me.

Lionel raised an eyebrow when I told him that I was going out again but said not a word. I drove toward the village when I reached the main gate, but only covered half that distance before turning onto one of the unpaved roads that ran out to some of the farms. I had not been this way before but the only turns were obviously leading to individual holdings and I had no difficulty in finding my way. All of the farms that I passed were in good repair and showed signs of recent activity except the very last one, where the house was boarded up and the barn looked as though it was slumping slightly to one side. I remembered from the lease information that a shift in the water table had rendered this particular area untenable.

The road ended there so I parked next to the house so that the car would not be easily spotted from the road, although there really was no reason to worry about that. I suppose I was caught up in the spirit of intrigue. In any case, I left the farm behind me quickly as I walked across the now tangled and untended fields toward a line of trees in the distance.

The map proved to be quite helpful from this point onward because several landmarks were labeled. The trees were not as densely packed as they had appeared originally and I was able to make my way fairly easily at first. Then the ground began to break up as pools of water appeared with increasing frequency. There were numerous dead trees, presumably drowned, and there was a constant sound of splashing water, which I discovered was caused by frogs. On one occasion I saw what appeared to be a snake, but it was only an oddly colored vine. I passed at least four sinkholes, but they were obvious from a distance and I made my way carefully around them.

I grew somewhat concerned after that because there were no longer any outstanding features to mark my way and the only guide I had was the direction of the sun. As I've mentioned, I'm not an outdoors type of person and my confidence waned rapidly. There was also an intermittent appalling stench which I assumed was the result of stagnant water and rotting foliage. Understanding the cause did not make the experience any less unpleasant.

Fortunately, by the time I began to grow actively anxious, I was close enough to my destination that I caught sight of it in the distance. It was the first of several raised mounds, all heavily overgrown so that I was never able to see more than one at a time, although I was able to determine that they were arranged more or less in a straight line. There was also a pool of thick, muddy water to which I gave a wide berth, assuming that this was yet another of the sinkholes I'd been warned about. I began to move very cautiously, testing the ground with each step before shifting my weight forward.

I reached the last of the mounds without incident, but also without making any real discovery. I climbed to the top of that one – sacrilegious though this might be – hoping for a better vantage point. That enabled me to see more trees, but nothing to justify my excursion.

I was on the verge of turning to begin the long walk back when I heard a sound that did not belong to nature. Something metallic had clinked against another object in the near distance. I had a general idea of the direction, which would take me even further away from civilization. Reaching into my pocket, I closed my hand over my pistol to reassure myself, and then set off to investigate, attempting to make as little noise as possible. I was not very successful and when I finally reached the shadow of a rocky ledge and saw the remains of what had obviously been a recent campfire, I had already unknowingly announced my presence.

The voice came from behind me. "I was wondering if you'd pay me a visit. Welcome to my humble and very temporary abode."

I turned in alarm, forgetting all about the weapon I carried, and found myself facing a tall, slender figure wrapped in a green cloak and wearing a peaked hat. This was unquestionably the person I had seen the night we chased Selden.

"Wanda!" I exclaimed. "What in the world are you doing out here?"

CHAPTER SEVENTEEN

Needless to say, I was dumbfounded. Apparently Wanda was nearly as surprised to see me.

"I never really expected to see you out wandering in the swamp." She stepped past me and I followed her into what turned out to be a small camp. There was a tent pitched in a cluster of bushes so cleverly that it was invisible until you were almost close enough to touch it. I could see a sleeping bag inside, lying across a bed of leaves and small branches. Just beyond was a knapsack, which had fallen over onto its side.

"How long have you been here?"

"I rented a car the day after you left and drove to Moran, just south of the valley, then hiked the rest of the way. However did you find me?" There was a fallen tree to one side of the tent and Wanda seated herself and crossed her arms.

"I knew there was someone else living out this way. Someone spotted your fire. You know about the escaped convict, I assume?"

She nodded. "I heard about it on the drive north, and there was talk of it in the village when I visited there."

"You bought food at the grocery."

"Yes, and a few other provisions. It made no sense to carry them all the way from Moran."

"I saw you out here one night, from a considerable distance. Obviously I had no idea who you were. And then one of the locals told me that he'd seen a fire out this way. He has a telescope. I suspected you might be our mystery man from Boston."

"And came out alone to beard him in his lair? That was taking quite a chance."

"I was careful, and I am armed."

"So I noticed. I am sorry not to have told you everything but I only decided on this course of action after you were gone, and it seemed best to avoid any contact with you after I'd arrived. So tell me what has happened at the Manor."

"I have detailed notes. There's been rather a lot of activity but I don't see how any of it puts us any forwarder."

"A summary will do for now. Most of what I have learned has been from the periphery while you were dwelling at the heart of the matter."

And so I recounted as best I could my experiences since arriving at Baskerville Manor. I'm afraid it was not the most organized presentation, and I had to backtrack from time to time to explain a detail that I had inadvertently omitted but which was relevant later in the narrative. Wanda asked only a couple of questions until I had finished, and then had me go over various portions of the story in more detail. The entire process took well over an hour.

When she was satisfied that she had thoroughly digested my information, Wanda provided a few revelations of her own. For one thing, Lydia Longtree was not completely unknown in the village. She was a friend of Dolores Staples and her brother and had visited them from time to time ever since Dolores bought the property two years earlier.

"I hadn't realized that Dolores was so new to the valley." I knew that her cousin was a latecomer, of course, since he had told me himself, but somehow I had assumed that she was a long term resident.

"She rented the house on an annual basis and renewed it after the first year. I have been unable to determine where her income derives other than what portion comes from renting a room to Dennis Staples, whose income comes reportedly from an arcane research and development company. I have made inquiries there, but they insist that all of their arrangements of this nature are confidential. They would not even confirm that Staples was employed by them. I have reason to believe that he is not."

"He's studying some sort of rare plant that might have esoteric properties. I never thought to ask what his cousin did for a living."

"Dolores is not his cousin. She's his wife. Their lineage is somewhat murky because they are were not born here, but they made no secret of their relationship when they entered the country and for some time afterward."

"Why would they conceal the truth?"

"It's possible to speculate but not very productive. She is noticeably darker in complexion than he is and there are still areas in this country where that would count against her. It may simply be that he wished to provide some distance to improve his own professional life. But I agree that it raises questions."

I was thoughtful for a moment. "I wonder if we could determine whether or not Dennis Staples was recently absent from the valley for two or three days."

Wanda nodded approvingly. "You suspect that he was the man we encountered in Boston."

"He has the same general build. He's clean shaven, but the beard could have been artificial or conjured. It might be difficult to prove that he was absent. Dolores would be in a position to testify that he had not done so, and he spends so much of his time in the swamps that it would be quite easy for him to be absent without anyone else being aware of it."

"And that would have been a very effective ruse. Fortunately for us, it didn't happen that way. The two of them left together. It appears that Dennis Staples has never learned to drive an automobile and is dependent upon his wife if he desires to travel any distance without recourse to public transportation. She drove him to Boston."

"Are you sure of that?" It was a foolish question. I have never known Wanda to state as a fact something that she hadn't confirmed.

"The postmistress was instructed to hold deliveries for the three days in question. She was most helpful when I expressed curiosity about her rather boring job. I also learned that a Mrs. Jenkins receives the largest number of mail order catalogues in the community, that Dr. James is a frequent recipient of registered mail, that Miss Lawrence and the tavern were being dunned for unpaid bills until fairly recently, and so forth. I'm afraid an appreciation of confidentiality is not one of Mrs. Barton's qualities."

"So they were both in Boston. And that suggests that Dolores was the author of the letter warning Sir Henry to return to England."

"Undoubtedly. In fact I have compared that document to copies of the local newspaper that is distributed in the local rural communities and the typeface is a perfect match. I believe she had already decided to deliver that warning before they ever left Vermont and had prepared the note in advance, waiting only for the opportunity to deliver it."

"So there is dissension between them."

"At least to some degree."

"And what is Lydia Longtree's role in all this?"

"That has yet to be determined. She may be entirely innocent, or she may have a personal agenda of her own which may or may not overlap with that of Dennis Staples."

"I am sure that she has designs on Sir Henry's money. Perhaps her intention is to marry him and then, with the collusion of Staples, murder her husband in such a way that she would inherit everything. That would leave her free to marry Staples, thereby rewarding them both."

"That's possible, although if I were in Staples' place, I wouldn't put much reliance on a plan that hinges upon trusting a deceitful woman to share her ill gotten gains after the deed was done. It seems even more likely that they are pursuing their avaricious plans independently. It may be that she attempted to induce Charles Baskerville to marry her, but realized that it was never going to happen."

"Then it would clearly be to her benefit for Charles to die so that she could make a play for the nephew."

"Precisely, Perry. We'll make a detective of you yet. And you have confirmed my suspicion that Longtree already knew Sir Henry long before he came to this country."

"She said that Charles suggested she pay a visit while she was in England."

"That might well be true, or she might just have learned of his existence and invented the story as a means of introducing herself to our client. With Charles dead, there would be no one in a position to contradict her version of events."

I sat for a few moments, digesting all of this. "Then you are convinced that this was murder and not some revenant curse?"

"I never believed in a magical cause for a moment. The major unanswered question, however, is how Staples plans to benefit from Sir Henry's death. While I cannot completely discount the idea that there is collusion between himself and Longtree, I find it inelegant. He has put too much careful planning into this to leave the eventual outcome to chance. And that makes the matter more urgent. If marriage to Longtree is part of the plan, then we have weeks if not months in which to work, because it would obviously spoil everything if he died before the wedding. On the other hand, if Longtree is not a co-conspirator, then Staples must act soon to remove her from the equation."

The sun was sinking and I suddenly became apprehensive about the journey back. Wanda correctly interpreted my sudden agitation. "Don't concern yourself. I know the way to civilization quite well now and we'll find our way with no difficulty."

"You're coming with me then?"

"Yes, I think so. This deception has outlived its usefulness. It will only take me a few minutes to pack things up and then we'll be off. I assume you have a vehicle waiting somewhere? I can't imagine walking all the way from the Manor unless it was necessary. I have done so on three occasions and it is not an experience I wish to repeat yet again."

I explained about the car I had borrowed. "Then you've been to the Manor. I imagine it was you that I spotted in the cemetery at some ungodly hour of the morning."

"So it was. And you must have been the one who scared me off. I had thought it was Lionel but I didn't stay around to check. I also saw you drive through the main gate on one occasion. I almost revealed myself to you then, but by the time I recognized who was driving, you had gone past and I was still reluctant to make my presence generally known."

"Do you know yet how Charles Baskerville was killed?"

"I think I have the general idea, but I'll keep that to myself for the time being, if you don't mind. There are still some details I need to work out and I hate being wrong."

The walk back to the car was, despite the heavy dusk, easier than I had expected. Wanda had found a slightly shorter and much less overgrown route and I happily allowed her to be our guide. It was full dark by the time we reached the car, bundled the tent and now fully stuffed knapsack into the back seat, and set off toward Baskerville Manor.

But it would be a while yet before we reached it.

We were just short of the paved road when two police cars rushed past with lights flashing heading south, followed almost immediately by an ambulance. I would have been turning to follow in any case since the Manor drive was in that direction but Wanda told me to follow the ambulance and so we did.

The cavalcade came to a stop only a half mile short of the valley rim. Two other vehicles were already there, a panel truck and a battered Triton station wagon. There was considerable confusion among the half dozen or so people milling around and no one questioned us when I pulled off the road and we continued forward on foot.

There were two men who were obviously outfitted to go hunting. I had been told that some of the farmers shot wild pheasants in the foothills but that this activity had been suspended while it was believed that Selden might be in the area. As we learned later, these two gentlemen had been frustrated by the informal ban and had come out to do some shooting far enough from the village that no one was likely to hear their gunfire.

One of them was speaking to a pair of police officers while the ambulance people unpacked their stretcher. The other hunter led two more officers off into the woods and Wanda and I followed at a short distance. No one objected to our presence but I assumed that this happy state of affairs would not continue indefinitely.

Wanda, however, has this gift of looking as though she belonged wherever it was that she happened to be. When the threesome ahead of us came to an abrupt halt, she didn't even slow down, just led me up to where they stood. It was the edge of a small clearing and, as I also learned later, part of a well known game trail that led from the valley up through a narrow cleft in the mountains to the outside world.

There was a slight depression ahead of us and we couldn't see much in the moonlight, but one of the police officers activated an illuminarium and cool, slightly blue tinted light washed through the area. There was a body lying face down in the depression, and at first glance I had the horrible feeling that it was Sir Henry. The clothing was his style, although not immediately familiar, and his general build was not totally dissimilar. But then I realized that this was a somewhat shorter man and that his hair had been cut close to his skull, unlike Sir Henry's full and somewhat shaggy style.

The second officer leaned down and slowly rolled the body over and I gasped, because I did recognize the man after all. I had only seen him once and at a distance in poor light, but there was no question whatsoever in my mind that this was Selden, the escaped convict.

My identification was made somewhat more difficult by the fact that there were ragged claw marks on his face. His throat had been similarly savaged and the front of his torso was black with dried blood. He had been dead for a considerable period of time, I realized, and the later scryopsy revealed that he had died sometime during the previous night, long before the two would-be hunters stumbled across his body and called for help.

I was thoroughly perplexed but when I glanced at Wanda, she was nodding to herself as though someone had just handed her the missing piece of a jigsaw puzzle and the solution was finally within her grasp.

CHAPTER EIGHTEEN

One of the officers was taking a belated interest in the two of us, but Wanda had apparently seen as much as she cared to. She touched my arm and indicated that we should return to the car. We did so without speaking and only when we were inside did I start asking the questions that I had been suppressing.

"What do you suppose happened, and why Selden?"

"I think he succumbed, after a fashion, to the same agency that was responsible for the death of Charles Baskerville."

"His throat was torn out!"

"Yes, the physical side of things went further this time. As to your second question, I believe that Selden's fate was sealed when he donned the garments of the late Charles Baskerville, as those almost certainly were."

I remembered Mrs. Lionel removing a bundle from the master bedroom at the Manor. "He would have been too easy to recognize in his prison clothing so the Lionels provided him with something more respectable."

"Good intentions gone awry, I'm afraid. Offhand, I would say that this was an accident, or at least that the villainous Mr. Staples did not plan for it to happen. It rather muddies the story that this was all the result of a family curse, given that Selden has no blood connection to the Baskervilles."

"Then you think that he has conjured up some magically empowered homunculus in the form of a hippogriff?"

"Possibly. He has certainly created the illusion of one to startle a few of the local people. But it was no illusion that killed Selden and even a homunculus cannot act outside its narrowly circumscribed purpose. I believe that a perfectly ordinary griffin would have done quite well, if it was suitably motivated."

"Griffins rarely attack people," I observed.

"Which is why I stipulated that it would have to have been motivated in some fashion. Let's return to the Manor. I think we're approaching the end game."

In fact we were, because Sir Henry had a guest. Two of them, in fact, for Dr. James was there along with Dennis Staples. They were in the library when we arrived and after identifying Wanda to Lionel, we made our way there. Sir Henry was wrapped in a robe and wore slippers, but he looked considerably better. Dr. James was admonishing him about something when we arrived while Staples sat quietly to one side, hands clasped, apparently deep in thought. I forced myself to greet him with a reasonable degree of warmth, despite my suspicion of his involvement in what was now a case of double murder.

Sir Henry looked quite pleased to see Wanda and started to rise from his seat, but Wanda insisted that he stay where he was.

"Lionel has disturbed Dr. James and insisted that he come up to examine me, and since Dennis was with him at the time he volunteered to come along and cheer me up. I've told them both that it was nothing and that I'm already on the mend, but the good doctor insists on prescribing something herbal that will undoubtedly taste so bad that it's worse than what it is supposed to cure."

"Alternatively you could come down to the clinic, out of the range of your suppression spell, and I could administer a more sophisticated potion." Dr. James did not seem at all cowed by Sir Henry's tone. "And it would be even more effective if you took better care of yourself. Running around in the swamp at night, drinking brandy on an empty stomach, gorging on Mrs. Lionel's admittedly marvelous but very rich foods, and so forth do not add up to a healthy lifestyle. They could be just as deadly as your fanciful family curse."

"There's been another tragedy," said Wanda. "A dead man has just been found out in the swamp."

All three men looked surprised and somewhat alarmed, including Staples. If he had been aware of Selden's death, he was a consummate actor.

"Who was it?" asked Dr. James.

I refrained from answering because I wasn't sure how Wanda wanted the conversation to proceed, but she identified him immediately. "He was apparently on his way out of the valley when something attacked him. His throat was torn out."

"The hippogriff!" Sir Henry was clearly alarmed.

"I don't think so," replied Wanda. "We examined the scene and there were no hoof prints. The ground was soft and would have taken an impression quite readily. I think we can rule out the Baskerville family bogey."

Staples stirred himself. "Aren't you a private investigator, Miss Coyne? I seem to have heard your name somewhere."

"I am surprised my reputation has extended this far, but you are correct. Sir Henry has employed me to look into his uncle's death."

"The state police investigated the incident quite thoroughly. I cannot imagine what you could possibly unearth after such a long interval. And the cause of death, after all, was heart failure. There was never any strong indication that a crime was committed."

"That is what I am here to determine."

I thought I sensed an almost physical tension between the two, but it was probably simply my imagination. I knew that Wanda believed that Staples was our man and that undoubtedly colored my perceptions. I didn't trust myself to speak unnecessarily because I feared I might say the wrong thing. In any case, I didn't need to be on my guard for long because Dr. James pronounced himself reasonably satisfied that Sir Henry was not about to expire on the spot and he and Staples soon took their leave.

"Your assistant has been most helpful, both in his assumed and in his concealed roles. So I hope that he will not feel belittled in any fashion when I admit that I feel better for your presence." Sir Henry offered us brandy and we both declined. After a momentary hesitation, he put the decanter back without having poured any for himself.

"He has provided a summary of your adventures during my absence. I must say, Sir Henry, that it was rather unwise of you to run around in the swamps searching for an escaped murderer."

"Yes, well, I've never been one to sit on the sidelines while others take the risks. And I fancy my motives did me credit even if my execution was deficient."

"That's as may be, but I want to caution you that your life almost certainly is in danger, if not immediately, then in the near future."

Sir Henry's face twisted. "You don't mean you think the curse is real after all?"

"No, or at least not in any arcane sense. I don't envy the Baskerville family its luck, however mundane the source of its problems."

"If there is a human agency, have you identified the man?"

"I believe so, but it is more in the nature of a conspiracy, I fear, and we need to be certain that we have caught all of the participants in our net before we show our hands."

"Who is it then?"

Wanda shook her head. "I urge you to let me keep that information confidential for the moment. As I've said you're in no immediate danger and I'm afraid that if you were told everything you would be unable to conceal your feelings and one or more of those who plot against you might take flight."

For a few seconds, Sir Henry looked as though he was going to argue the point, but at last he nodded. "You're probably right. I've never been one to suffer fools or turn the other cheek to my enemies. I place myself in your hands, at least for the time being. But if the contest requires a bit of acting on my part, rest assured that I am capable of a little deceit in a good cause."

Mrs. Lionel was advised that we would have another guest. I doubt it would inconvenience her more than slightly since she always made enough food to feed us twice over. Wanda was given the very room in which we'd surprised Lionel signaling to Selden, but there was no reason for him to be making any further nocturnal visits.

Sir Henry rang for Lionel and quietly told him about Selden's death. "Please convey our sympathies to your wife when you tell her. And she needn't fuss over supper this evening. We can make do with leftovers or I might even dress myself so that we can drive into the village. The Tavern does a good sandwich."

Lionel thanked him and insisted that Mrs. Lionel would want to carry on as usual. In fact she served a quite nice pot roast and while her eyes were red she seemed otherwise unaffected. There was little conversation during the meal and afterward we retired to the sitting room where Wanda read my accumulated notes while we all sipped brandy. Sir Henry, I noticed, nursed his own drink and when it was gone, refrained from having another.

Sir Henry in fact seemed increasingly restless and he eventually broke the silence abruptly. "I have to tell you something, Miss Coyne, which I have heretofore kept to myself. It is somewhat private but the suspicions that your statements have aroused in me make it imperative that I speak out. Although I have not been to

America before this trip, I do have another connection here which is perhaps relevant. Several months ago, I received a visitor, a woman who formerly lived not far from here. She was an acquaintance of my uncle Charles and when she announced her intention of visiting England for a prolonged stay, he insisted that she pay a visit to Baskerville Hall. Or at least, that is her version of events."

Wanda leaned forward, intending to speak, but Sir Henry pushed on quickly. "As it happens, we became quite fond of each other and she spent a good portion of her visit as my guest. When it came time for her to return, I found that I was actively distressed at the prospect of her absence and I was in fact contemplating a trip of my own as soon as I could deal with certain financial problems with which I was then wrestling. My uncle's death obviously hurried my timetable. I have since spoken to her by telephone on more than one occasion and we have met once. I am quite frankly considering asking the woman to be my wife."

"That would be Miss Longtree," said Wanda, taking advantage of a momentary pause.

Sir Henry was clearly taken aback. "You know of the lady?"

"Only in the abstract. I have not yet made her acquaintance."

"Yes, well, you see my question is whether or not you think she is a part of this conspiracy. I am not a stupid man. I realize that she stands to gain a great deal by marrying me, but that argues that she certainly would not be a party to a murder that would reduce her prospects. I am frankly befuddled by this entire situation. Can you at least tell me if you have reason to believe that she is involved?"

Wanda hesitated, choosing her words carefully. "I know nothing to her discredit, Sir Henry, and have no evidence that she was a party to the murder of your uncle, or that she has any nefarious plans involving your own life. That said, I must consider the possibility that she is indeed involved, perhaps in some manner not readily apparent, perhaps quite innocently. I have nothing detrimental to say about her at this time, but I also fear that I cannot set your mind at ease. There are aspects of this case that I do not yet understand."

Our client looked mildly relieved. "That's something, at least. I do hope you'll be able to clear this up. I find it very stressful to consider that I am at the center of a sinister plot and that there is virtually no one whom I can trust."

Wanda assured him she believed a conclusion to the case was imminent.

"Have you learned the identity of the man who shadowed us in Boston?"

"Yes, I have, and I believe I also know what happened to your missing shoes. The bearded man took both of them, of course."

"That seems to me the oddest part of the entire situation. Whatever reason could justify risking exposure for an innocuous item of clothing? And why take two of them on two separate occasions?"

"That at least I can answer for you. The first theft had a definite, rational purpose. Unfortunately, the stolen shoe proved to be deficient and that made the second theft necessary."

"But they were both just shoes! What possible value could they have, and what possible difference existed between them?"

"The difference, Sir Henry, was that the first shoe stolen was brand new and had never been worn. The second was well broken in."

CHAPTER NINETEEN

For the first time in my experience, it was Sir Henry who first retired for the night. Although he looked a good deal better than he had earlier in the day, I imagine he was still not feeling himself and I suspected that Dr. James had given him something which would make him sleepy. In any case, Wanda and I were left alone in the library where we sat in complete silence for so long that I was contemplating my own bed when she spoke.

"Staples has remarkable self control. He showed only an understandable degree of surprise when he heard of Selden's death, although I very much doubt that was any part of his plan. It renders the Baskerville curse moot, given that Selden was not a member of the family, and suggests that the plot which he has put into motion has escaped his control."

"Do you think he has a confederate? His sister or Miss Longtree perhaps? They might have acted without his knowledge or approval."

Wanda shook her head. "I am still not absolutely certain of the identity of Staples' partner, or partners."

"The police are not going to be happy with us if we withhold information."

She stirred slightly in her chair. "And what would we tell them? We have nothing to prove the case against Staples. No, I think we need to be patient a bit longer. If Staples has indeed lost his grip on events, then it won't be long before something slips through the cracks and we will have the proof we need. But to set your mind at ease, I have already provided an abbreviated version of my theory to a sympathetic ear among the state police."

We went upstairs together shortly after that and one thing of note occurred as we mounted the steps. I don't think that I have mentioned in this account that the front hall and staircase were liberally decorated with portraits of the Baskerville family running back for at least two centuries. Most were men, of course, but there were women as well. There were individual variations but the majority of them were clearly related to Sir Henry. The family resemblance was quite strong.

We were halfway up when Wanda paused and regarded those nearest to us in the dim light. "Sometimes, Perry, the solution to a convoluted problem lies in the simplest of devices, and the most obscure and seemingly distant of them proves to be quite near at hand. Look at that fellow, just above the portrait of the lady with the cat in her lap."

I followed his eyes and identified the portrait in question. It was labeled Ronald Baskerville, born in 1870, died in 1921. His expression was solemn, suggesting boredom, and he looked vaguely familiar to me. The setting was easily identifiable as the sitting room downstairs. Even the furniture was the same. "A member of the American branch of the family," I said.

"Yes, but more than that. Look again, not for the detail but taken as a whole."

I did as instructed and after a few seconds I realized what Wanda was trying to point out. "He looks a great deal like Dennis Staples."

"My feeling exactly. The family resemblance is remarkable. A major piece of the puzzle has just fallen to us."

I realized the implications immediately. "Then he is potentially heir to the Baskerville fortune. At least he is if he's legitimate. I have no idea what the legal status of bastards might be."

"It depends upon the laws of inheritance here in Vermont, I imagine, as well as the specific terms of Sir Henry's will and the structure of the family trust."

"Apparently he has no will. He has been deferring it pending the outcome of his wooing of Miss Longtree." I had failed to mention this earlier so it came as a surprise.

Wanda shook her head. "A foolish choice given the circumstances. He must rectify that situation immediately, even if he finds himself tearing it up in favor of a new arrangement if his suit is successful."

"Is this enough to take to the police?"

"Not quite. But it may have given us the leverage we need to act decisively and bring this to a conclusion. Sleep well tonight, Perry, because tomorrow will likely be a very busy day."

The following morning we said and did nothing of consequence until breakfast was over and done with. Wanda suggested that we move to the library and there, after overcoming some resistance, she convinced Sir Henry that it was imperative that he immediately draw up a will. "I realize that it will not necessarily reflect your ultimate wishes, but in the event that our plans miscarry, it will at least ensure that there is no possible way for the villain to succeed you."

I typed up a very simple will leaving the English property to the Peters cousin, with the balance to be split evenly among three charities. The individual farms would go to their respective tenants. "I really should provide for the servants."

"And so you shall." I added a few quick codicils.

He signed and we witnessed it, then placed it in his desk. "Should I take this to mean that you are not as confident as you might be that I will survive?"

Wanda took the question seriously. "We will be taking every possible step for your safety commensurate with the need to bring this reign of terror to an end. The alternative to taking some risk is to leave the initiative entirely with your enemy."

"I see your point. All of this putting my affairs in order smacks of the closing chapters of my personal story."

"Then we shall all hope for a sequel."

But it was obvious that the situation was preying on his mind because he grew unusually restless and then excused himself to make a telephone call. When he returned, he was in considerably better spirits. "I have a luncheon engagement at the tavern in the village."

"Mrs. Lionel is going to think we don't like her cooking," I quipped.

"No fear of that. The two of you will undoubtedly be well fed."

Obviously we were not invited to accompany him. "Do you think that it's wise for you to go there alone?" I asked.

"I doubt the confounded creature will attack me in broad daylight while I'm traveling in a car. I appreciate your consideration – both of you – but I can't spend my life hiding indoors."

As I've mentioned, Wanda is a shrewd judge of people and their moods. She made no attempt to dissuade him, but did caution him to keep his eyes open. "I don't expect you'll be in any particular danger but it's best to be on guard."

"Can you at least tell us whom you're meeting?" I asked.

But it was Wanda who answered. "Unless I'm mistaken, Sir Henry is off to have it out with Miss Longtree."

Sir Henry nodded. "I won't reveal anything you've told me in confidence, but I shall insist upon an answer to my proposal."

I was concerned that he might thereby disrupt Wanda's plans, but short of revealing some of the information which we had so far withheld, I could think of no way to dissuade him. Wanda, in fact, apparently looked upon the enterprise favorably.

"I don't see any reason why you should not. At the least, it will remove an element of uncertainty from the equation. I wish you the best of luck."

Wanda requested a tour of the grounds and Sir Henry was glad to oblige. I could not resist commenting out of his hearing that I imagined Wanda was probably already quite familiar with them. "Ah, but I haven't seen them in the daylight. In the darkness, it's another world entirely."

It was a warm, damp morning, and there were still pockets of fog, the thickest I'd seen since arriving. There was a kind of haze hovering over the swamp and the overcast sky made it all blur into an unbroken expanse of dull grey. Neither Wanda nor Sir Henry seemed troubled by the gloom, however. Sir Henry was positively buoyant, perhaps because he had decided to force the issue of his romantic entanglement with Lydia Longtree. For his sake, I hoped that I was wrong about her intentions, and that she was at worst an innocent pawn in the hands of Staples.

We visited Charles Baskerville's grave where we paused a moment respectfully. Sir Henry pointed out the place where his uncle had fallen dead, but Wanda expressed only polite interest. I knew her well enough to realize that she was deep in thought, answering remarks addressed to her automatically, with only a portion of her mind. I knew as well that she would not reveal what she was planning until it was absolutely necessary. It was not that she was by nature secretive, but rather that she so richly hated being wrong that she kept her own counsel until the last possible moment.

We returned to the Manor where Sir Henry excused himself and went to his room. I heard him drawing a bath and realized that he would be off to the village within the hour. We had spent more time on our grand tour than I had realized and it was closing in on midday. I ventured to mention my concerns about Sir Henry and this solitary undertaking but Wanda seemed imperturbable. "He's a grown man, Perry. We can hardly insist that he take no risk whatsoever. And Staples is a careful planner. He is unlikely to take advantage of a spontaneous decision on Sir Henry's part unless forced by circumstances to do so. In fact, that's the trait we must exploit."

But she wouldn't suggest how that might be achieved.

Freshly attired and groomed, Sir Henry was as cheerful as I'd ever seen him when he set off in the car. Mrs. Lionel had prepared an elaborate salad and some sliced meat and despite my apprehensions, I ate more than usual. I fancied that I'd already gained a couple of pounds since arriving at Baskerville Manor. Julia would want to know what I'd been eating in her absence.

The next two hours were among the longest in my lifetime. Wanda announced her intention of taking a short nap and disappeared into her room. I wandered into the library in search of another book to read and selected one, but I read the first few pages three times before realizing that I could not concentrate. I eventually went to my own room and lay down, but the thoughts and memories passing through my mind were so volatile that I was unable to sleep for a long time, though I finally dozed off.

Sir Henry had not returned by mid-afternoon when I rose and came downstairs. Wanda was in the den, reading a collection of short stories by William Fryer Harvey. The sky outside was lighter, but the cloud cover was unbroken.

"Is he back yet?" I asked as I slumped into another chair.

"There's been no sign of him." Wanda still sounded as though she didn't have a worry in the world.

A few minutes later I heard a car drive up to the front of the house. "That'll be him now." I rose and started out of the room.

"Perhaps." Wanda followed me to the front door, which Lionel was just opening as we arrived. Through the gap I could see a dark blue Rambler roadster, nothing like the one Sir Henry was driving. A second vehicle, a Fjord Viking, pulled up behind it.

"I'll take care of this, Lionel," said Wanda. "These gentlemen are here to see me."

The Rambler turned out to be the vehicle that Wanda had rented and stored in Moran. She had called that morning to arrange for it to be delivered to the Manor. She tipped both drivers, who got into the Viking and followed the driveway around its circle and left the way they had come. "I think we'll have need of our own means of transportation today, Perry. And the car was doing us no good in a garage in Moran."

The Viking had barely disappeared when Sir Henry returned. He was smiling broadly when he stepped out of the car. "I take it the lady has accepted," said Wanda.

"Indeed she has. No date has been set because I hope to have this other matter cleared up beforehand. I cannot believe that she is a part of the conspiracy against me, but I would be a foolish man indeed if I did not accept the possibility that I am being deceived."

"That's excellent news," said Wanda. "And might I make a suggestion of an appropriate way to celebrate the event?"

"By all means."

"I noticed that the Black Goat Tavern has a small, private function room. It would seem to me that an engagement dinner would be just the thing."

Sir Henry looked pleased. "That seems a capital idea. I will have to see if the space is available in the near future, perhaps this coming weekend."

"Actually, I called Miss Lawrence during your absence in anticipation of the happy news. It is in fact available tonight."

Our host suddenly appeared uncertain. "That's rather soon, isn't it? Lydia is already on her way home."

"It's only a half hour drive, isn't it? And she would want to change clothes for the event in any case."

"Well, I suppose that's true." He seemed to warm to the idea. "But I know so few people here. I haven't even met Mrs. James yet, and none of the farmers except Lafter."

"I suggest that you call and invite Lafter and the doctor and his wife, and Mr. Staples and his cousin. And Miss Lawrence herself if you'd like. That would make a party of eight."

Sir Henry nodded, then frowned. "I make it ten."

"You have undoubtedly included Perry and I. As much as we are honored by the thought, I doubt that it would be appropriate to include employees, which is what we are. And in any case, I have had my car delivered here because Perry and I must absent ourselves from the valley this evening. We will return sometime in the late morning tomorrow."

"Both of you will be gone?"

"Unfortunately it is necessary. You will be in no danger if you do precisely what I ask." Her voice had sudden become heavy with meaning.

Not a stupid man, Sir Henry realized that something was afoot. "What do you want me to do?"

"I understand that you are fond of hiking."

"I believe I am as fit as any man my age."

"There is a trail that starts from the eastern edge of the village, not far from the Tavern in fact, which leads to this property by a direct route. It is in fact approximately half the distance of a trip by car."

"I have seen it marked on one of my uncle's maps. It skirts along a rough spot of land near the rim of the valley."

"The walk takes somewhat less than an hour in daylight, perhaps a bit more in the darkness. It would be very helpful if you allowed us to drop you off at the Tavern on our way out of the valley and that you walk home afterward using that route. I stress the importance of not varying from that path."

Sir Henry chuckled. "You're not really leaving us, are you? You want to use me as bait for our killer."

For just a second Wanda seemed uncertain, but she made a quick decision. "I assure you that you will be perfectly safe."

"Nothing is perfectly safe where murder is concerned, but don't worry, I'm not a cowardly man. If it is necessary to take a risk in order to put all of this behind me, then that is exactly what I will do."

"With luck, sir, this will all be over with before morning."

"One way or another, eh?" He laughed shortly. "I assume that I am to announce both your absence and my intention to walk home during the dinner party?"

"That would be most helpful."

"Which means that someone there is responsible for the death of my uncle."

"So I believe."

"And you will spring your trap on this individual before the night is out."

"If the situation I anticipate develops, then we almost certainly will do just that."

"Then how can I refuse? I suppose I should start making telephone calls."

Happily everyone invited accepted, although Liz Lawrence stressed that she would be in and out, depending upon the number of customers in the bar proper.

When he was done making arrangements and had left the den, I heard Wanda call the state police and ask to speak to Captain Lester.

CHAPTER TWENTY

I felt considerably better after hearing Wanda's side of the conversation with the state police. This wasn't going to be solely our responsibility any longer. I had the impression that Captain Lester wasn't entirely happy with the arrangements that Wanda had made but he ultimately agreed to them.

"There's one nagging little question that I hope to resolve next, Perry. Let's go have a visit with Miss Longtree."

I sat behind the wheel. Wanda obviously had a license but I knew from experience that she didn't enjoy driving. We took a slight detour so that she could show me the beginning of the trail from the village to the Manor grounds. It ran alongside a small cemetery and disappeared into a dense patch of spruce trees just beyond, but she assured me she had walked it herself and that it was well marked and maintained.

Longtree's home and business were both in Celador, which wasn't much larger than Grimalkin and was located close to the prison complex, although the latter was tastefully hidden from view. We took a few minutes to look around the shop, which specialized in handcrafts. A bored looking young woman was the only staff in evidence and there were no customers.

From there we went to Lydia Longtree's home, the address of which was readily available in the phone book. It was a rather small house, though well kept, and a car was parked snugly in the driveway. Hex signs were mounted on the outside walls but I couldn't tell if they were decorative or functional. There was a profusion of flowers in the yard, but they looked as though they could have used some pruning.

Longtree either didn't like or couldn't afford a door guardian so we used an old fashioned brass knocker to announce our presence. She answered the door promptly and recognized me instantly. Her eyes narrowed and I remembered that we had not parted friends. Wanda introduced herself as a detective employed by Sir Henry Baskerville. "Would it be possible for us to ask for a few minutes of your time? I know this sounds melodramatic but the future of more than one person – yourself included – may depend upon our having a conversation."

She expressed a welcome she obviously did not feel and we were ushered inside. The interior was clean and pleasant but I thought rather cluttered. The walls and every available surface were covered with craftswork, pottery, carvings in wood and stone, embroideries, blown glass, small paintings, hand wrought amulets, and so forth. We were offered chairs in a small sitting room which we accepted, and cold drinks, which we declined.

Wanda wasted no time on small talk. "We know that you have a relationship with Dennis Staples. In view of your recent commitment to Sir Henry Baskerville, we need to clear the air."

"And by what right do you question me, Miss Coyne? My private life is none of your concern."

"I am employed to protect the life of your fiancé, Miss Longtree. I can't imagine why you would want to do anything to interfere with that task."

She didn't appear to be at all mollified. "Perhaps, but I think I shall take this up with Henry this evening."

"I understand your hesitation. I wish I could be there personally to explain myself, but unfortunately my companion and I will not be able to return to the valley until tomorrow."

For a few seconds I thought we had reached an impasse. "There is no reason why I shouldn't answer. Dennis and I are friends, have been for some time. We even considered a formal alliance at one time."

"He asked you to marry him?" Wanda sounded surprised.

"Not in so many words, but we were moving in that direction. Both of us had second thoughts, however."

"How much do you know of his background?"

"We talked of our pasts, of course, but I will have to decline to discuss the specifics of his history. You will have to ask him yourselves."

"And we might do just that eventually. Are you certain that he considered marriage?"

"As certain as one could be without the actual words being spoken."

"That is most peculiar," said Wanda, "given the fact that he already has a wife."

A variety of emotions crossed Longtree's face in rapid succession. "That's not true. He would have told me."

Wanda shook her head. "I'm afraid it is. He is married to Dolores Staples, born Dolores Cruz."

Disbelief chased all other emotions away. "Dolores is his cousin, not his wife!"

"I am afraid that you have been deceived, Miss Longtree. I have confirmed this through the state police. They lived as man and wife when they first arrived in this country. He was already a citizen because his father was American, but Dolores went through the naturalization process."

Longtree slowly recovered herself. "Well, I suppose it's just as well then that we parted ways. I suppose that it is an unhappy marriage and that he considered a flirtation as a harmless pleasure. I cannot say that I was heartbroken when we brought it to an end, and of course I am immensely better off now."

Wanda reached into a pocket and extracted a folded piece of paper. "Would you look at this please?"

She took the note, which I recognized as the one I had found behind the library desk. "This is my handwriting."

"But you told my friend here that you did not write to Charles Baskerville on the night of his death."

"I didn't, or any other night." She frowned in concentration. "And I never drew this map either. This is almost certainly a note I sent to Dennis. His cousin – or rather his wife as I know now – had taken an aversion to me when it became obvious that Dennis and I were attracted to one another so I never called upon him at the house after that." She peered at the note again. "The date is not written in my hand. It was added after the fact, I believe."

She handed the note back to Wanda, who examined it briefly. "I agree, Miss Longtree. I suspected some sort of ruse but I couldn't be certain that you weren't a party to it."

"I had nothing to do with the death of Charles Baskerville."

"Certainly not intentionally, no. May I ask, was there any sort of romantic attraction between the two of you?"

"Charles and I?" Longtree laughed loudly. "Some detective you are. Did it never occur to you to wonder why Charles never remarried? He was as gay as they come, a charming man in many ways and without a single mean bone in his body, but he had no interest in the opposite sex. He only married Louise because he believed it was his duty to provide a male heir but I knew her well

154

and she confided in me that it was a marriage in name only, that he was unable to consummate it and stopped trying very quickly."

Wanda apologized for the intrusion and thanked her for having agreed to see us. We left a few minutes later after Wanda cautioned Longtree not to reveal that she knew the truth about Dennis at the evening's celebration. "It is important that we not disturb the status quo just yet. Everything will be explained later. I assure you it is essential to Sir Henry's safety."

"I'm not a giddy girl who can't keep her secrets, but I confess I'll be watching Dennis closely. Dolores as well."

As soon as we pulled out onto the street, I remarked that we had misjudged Longtree. "It looks like her motives are pure."

Wanda laughed at me. "Your original appraisal was correct, Perry. She's after Sir Henry's money and has been from the start. She is not, however, part of a conspiracy to murder him. Quite the contrary, in fact."

"Then why hasn't Staples long since cut her loose?"

"Because she was his insurance. If his plans went awry and he was unable to bring about Sir Henry's death in the short run, then he would wait until they were married before delivering the fatal blow. He could then either marry Miss Longtree, if she was amenable, and arrange for her to have an accident of her own, or if she decided against a formal liaison, he could revert to his original plan, kill her, and then lay claim to the estate."

"But surely it would go to Longtree's relatives under those circumstances."

"The legal issues are not clear because the Baskerville estate is a trust, but the question is moot because Longtree too is the last of her line. She has no living relatives. In any case, Staples would grasp at whatever straws remained."

We drove back to Grimalkin without exchanging more than a few words. I was mentally reviewing everything I thought I knew about the case based on Longtree's revelations. It was obvious now that Staples was indeed behind it all, but when I thought about it I realized that Wanda was correct that we lacked proof. We had virtually nothing that could be used to make a legal case against him.

At Wanda's direction we stopped at the Tavern. It was technically open, but there were no customers inside. The young man I'd seen once before was sweeping and he told us Liz was in back and that he'd tell her we were there. She came out wearing an apron, cleaning her hands with a dish towel. I started to introduce Wanda but it was unnecessary. "We've met. I stopped in for a drink once or twice. It gets pretty chilly out in the swamp at night. Irish Coffee is an admirable palliative." Wanda explained that she was a private investigator looking into the death of Charles Baskerville and that she'd like to ask a couple of questions.

"Go ahead. I liked Charles." We all sat at a table in the back.

"I understand that you sent a note to the Manor on the day of his death."

"That's right. I wanted to meet with him about a personal issue. I had Billy deliver it to him personally."

Wanda produced the note again. "May I assume that this was not the note you sent?"

Liz gave it a quick glance. "Nope. Not my handwriting and the paper is wrong. I wrote it on the back of a blank bar tab. The date is right, but the time is wrong."

I metaphorically kicked myself. I had never asked what time she had asked to meet with Charles.

"I couldn't have gone up to the Manor at eight. That's our busiest time. I asked him to meet me at the small gate at two o'clock. But then I knocked Mrs. Ardmore down." She repeated her story about the trip to the emergency room and its aftermath. "Is any of this important?"

Wanda put the note away. "Not really, but it was a distraction that needed to be resolved. May I ask if you have had any further difficulty with Mr. Doyle? I understand he has been harassing you of late."

Liz broke out into a really wonderful smile. "Haven't you been listening to the news? He was just indicted on multiple accounts of corruption including using compulsion spells to influence members of the legislature. I think he's going to be far too busy for the foreseeable future to bother me."

Liz went back to her kitchen duties and Wanda and I returned to the car. "Where now?" I asked.

"It's time for us to be seen leaving the valley. Why don't we swing by the post office so I can check general delivery and mention to Mrs. Barton that we're on our way north. She will have the news spread all over the village before we're out of sight."

We did drive north out of Grimalkin, and almost all the way to the rim of the valley. At the very last intersection, Wanda directed me to turn left onto a dirt road that led to a good sized farm house surrounded by poplars. As we drove into the yard, two men emerged from the house. One of them opened the barn door and waved for me to park the car inside. A police van was already there. The other man turned out to be Captain Lester of the Vermont State Police.

We shook hands all around and went inside where four uniformed policeman were sitting in the kitchen playing cards. The farmer was Albert Lester, the captain's brother and temporary recruit into our little conspiracy.

"Make yourself comfortable, Perry," said Wanda. "We're all going to stay out of sight here until dark."

CHAPTER TWENTY ONE

As soon as it was reasonably dark, we all climbed into the two concealed vehicles and drove back toward the village, but with our headlights off, relying on a pair of Surepath Charms that Captain Lester had brought along. Just short of the village proper, we turned onto another dirt road, passed two more farms, and finally parked in a meadow which was screened from town by a line of tall poplars. Then we set off on foot.

It took about twenty minutes to reach the woods on the east end of town and quietly make our way through them until we intersected the trail that Sir Henry was to take later in the evening. Speaking only in monosyllables until we were some distance away, we followed the trail, which rose steadily but at a reasonably gentle angle. Another twenty minutes took us to an outlook where we could look down at the village without being visible from below.

"Watch the top right window of the Tavern," Wanda told me in a low voice. "Liz will put a light there when Sir Henry leaves."

Captain Lester was dispersing his men into cover, working quietly and efficiently."

"You think this is where the attack will be?" I asked.

"Here or on the immediate approach. The rest of the trail is covered with trees. It's remotely possible that a griffin could fly along under the branches, but its nature is to dive on its prey from above. Charles Baskerville was out in the open, and so was the unfortunate Mr. Selden. And the attack wouldn't be too close to the village because Staples cannot take the risk that someone might witness it."

"Surely he doesn't seriously think that the authorities would accept that the family curse was responsible."

"I'm not convinced that Staples is entirely sane himself. He may believe that he is acting as an instrument of the curse. Even if he's sane, he probably hopes that the possibility will create enough confusion to confound the investigation."

I glanced at my wristwatch. "What time do you think they'll wind things up?"

"Oh, I would guess another hour or so before the party is over, and at least another thirty minutes for Sir Henry to walk this far. I would look for a comfortable spot to sit if I were you."

158

Unfortunately there was one factor that Wanda had not anticipated. The heavy fog of the previous day had returned and with a vengeance. The swamp was already swathed in a soft, dark cloud and the edges were rolling toward us making quite visible progress. Barely a third of our waiting time had passed before we could see wisps just a few feet below our current position.

"This is rather unfortunate," said Wanda. "I had assumed that we were high enough that the fog would not be troublesome. Maybe there is something to the family curse after all." I was sure this last was said in jest, but there was a note of concern in her voice.

I kept checking the time, convinced my watch was broken. The minutes could not possibly be passing so slowly. The advance of the fog had slowed but had not stopped and it drifted in billows around our feet. And then, finally, a light appeared in the window of the Tavern. I felt rising excitement and stirred restlessly. I knew that Lester and his men were close by, but I had not heard anything for quite a while and none were visible. Wanda slipped off to alert them that the game was underway, but I had no idea how she would locate them. The fog was by now waist high.

We were well outside the protective barrier at Baskerville Manor. The attack need not be purely mundane. Could Staples have conjured up some sort of hippogriff homunculus? If so, would it be vulnerable to the weapons carried by Lester's men? Wanda hadn't returned so I couldn't ask if she'd anticipated this possibility, but I told myself that she was too smart to have overlooked such an obvious complication. Intellectually, I remained quite confident, but my pulse was rapid and I felt a rush of anxiety. Not to mention that the fog was still rising, although almost imperceptibly now.

After what seemed an eternity, Wanda rejoined me. We were crouched on a small knoll that rose slightly above the path, screened from view by some brambles which would not have been sufficient in the daylight but which provided an adequate screen in the darkness, particularly with the fog acting as a mixed blessing. "It should be soon now," she whispered, and in fact it was almost immediately thereafter that I heard a sound from below.

Sir Henry appeared as little more than a blob of thicker fog, and in fact I could not have said at the time that it was he. The figure was holding something in one hand which I eventually realized was a makeshift walking stick. He had probably picked it up because the fog made it impossible to see the ground underfoot and he was quite evidently probing ahead cautiously as he advanced. He would reach us in another five minutes at his current pace.

The attack, when it came, was sudden and shocking and almost silent. I heard the faintest hint of a thrumming sound and then a dark shape fell past us and toward Sir Henry. The speed of the thing was so great that Captain Lester and his men did not react quickly enough to prevent its first strike, but Sir Henry had been forewarned and must have expected something of the kind, because he raised his staff just in the nick of time, flailing it at an attacker he must have sensed but not seen.

Wanda flashed past me and I belatedly followed. There were shouts and I heard Captain Lester's voice and then a pair of flashes as two firearms were discharged, one by Wanda and the other by Lester himself as I subsequently learned. There was a sudden screech of pain and fury so loud that it hurt my ears and I staggered. The dark shape rose into the air and I saw the outline of one of its wings against the clear sky before a fusillade of shots crashed. The shape jerked violently, faltered, and then fell with a crash into the brambles.

"Quickly now," said Lester. "The creature's master must be lurking close by."

Several figures emerged from their hiding places and started down the trail. Lester stopped one of them and gave instructions that the fallen creature be secured. "It's evidence," he told his subordinate, who probably with considerable reluctance began to force his way through the underbrush. But it was true. A forensic scryopsy would almost certainly reveal its association with its master.

I reached Sir Henry, who was out of breath but unharmed. "The beast bit off more than it could chew," he told me, but his breath was short and he clearly had had a fright. There was shouting from below and then more shots were fired, followed by a general uproar. I was reluctant to leave Sir Henry alone, but he urged me to go. "Make sure the villain doesn't escape. I'll be fine once I catch my breath."

So I started down the trail.

With six of us pursuing, one might think that it would have been a relatively easy task to apprehend Staples. If it had not been for that damnable fog, he might well have been captured long before he reached the end of the trail. Unfortunately, as we descended the fog swirled up and over our heads and we were soon floundering about. Staples, who was more familiar with the terrain, was far less hindered and was probably already in the village by the time we had gathered ourselves together and were making an organized descent.

We went immediately to the house where he had been staying. There were no lights on and no one answered the door, so Lester had two of his men break it down. Wanda and I remained outside while they checked the interior and after a few very tense moments, the lights were on and we were invited to enter.

Dolores Staples was lying on the kitchen floor. She had been knocked unconscious, according to her later testimony after she had objected too strenuously to her husband's plan. Her objection was, I have always believed, due less to her sense of humanity than to her fear of exposure, but this theme would later be offered as mitigation of her own crimes. Dr. James was summoned to deal with her while the house was thoroughly searched.

The basement proved to be very interesting. There was a large cage, currently unoccupied, with very thick bars, just the sort of thing to use to contain a griffin. A refrigerator stocked with raw meat stood nearby. There was also a straw dummy that vaguely resembled Sir Henry. A single shoe was tucked into its waistband, a shoe which was later identified as the one stolen from the hotel room in Boston.

"He needed something with Sir Henry's scent," explained Wanda. "The first one he stole was brand new and wouldn't serve, so he had to purloin another. I imagine he used magic to give the dummy Sir Henry's appearance – and before that the likeness of Charles Baskerville – and tormented the beast in some fashion to overcome its natural aversion to attacking humans."

We also found a pair of boots fashioned with horseshoes on the bottom, just the thing for leaving hoof prints without going to the trouble of finding a horse or unicorn to make them. There was a large chest inside of which lay the remains of a mechanical hippogriff, partially disassembled.

"Staples doubtless originally planned to use this to attack Charles Baskerville because he was unaware at that time of the protective spell at the Manor. I imagine he must have been quite surprised when he tried to introduce it in its animated form to the Manor grounds, only to have it fall inert when it touched the barrier. Staples probably had to disassemble it and make multiple trips to bring it back. He did manage to scare a few of the local people though, perhaps by intent, perhaps simply while practicing his control."

When we went back upstairs, Dr. James had managed to restore Dolores to consciousness, although she seemed both shaken and cowed. Lester asked her where her husband was and for a few minutes it seemed she would not answer. It was only when he formally arrested her on a charge of murder and conspiracy to commit murder that she began to cooperate.

"He's gone into the swamp. He has a hidey hole there. I don't know where it is."

"If he's in the swamp in this fog," said Dr. James, "then he probably won't be coming out. No matter how familiar he is with the area, he's more likely to end up in a sinkhole than at his destination. The rain we've had recently will make the entire area a potential deathtrap."

"He's too smart for that," said Dolores, pride in her husband overcoming her reluctance to betray him. "He'll have taken a Surepath with him."

Captain Lester had brought his own Surepath from the car, but while it would keep us safe if we conducted a search, it would not lead us to Staples. "He could cross the mountains at any of several points," complained Lester. "It would take a small army to seal off the entire swamp, and we couldn't raise one in time even if I could justify it."

He and Wanda seemed resigned to at least a temporary escape, but Dr. James spoke up. "I might be able to help with that. I happen to have a very good bloodhound in my kennel. All we need is a sample of his clothing, preferably something recently worn."

And that is how we ended up plunging into the swamp, Wanda and I, Dr. James, Lester, and two of his men. The other two were variously looking after Dolores Staples and the body of the griffin, which had been successfully recovered.

It was a nightmarish episode. The fog was so thick I could almost feel it pressing against my body. Lester and Dr. James led the way, or rather the hound led the way, with the rest of us struggling along behind. Lester's charm kept us away from the sinkholes and other dangers, but the hound was almost as adept at sensing them and we advanced more quickly than I expected.

The hound did not bark but a party of our size could hardly advance without making considerable noise and there was little doubt that Staples would hear us coming. He may have panicked when he realized that the perils of the foggy swamp were not dissuading us from our pursuit, because he doubled back on his own trail and set about ambushing us. Had we been two or three, this tactic might have succeeded and in fact he did manage to wound one of the uniformed officers when he opened fire. But the fog worked to our advantage on this occasion. He had not been able to see us clearly in the fog – his charm could not help him there. And the flashes of light when he fired were clearly visible to us.

I think everyone fired, including myself. There was a short, sharp cry of pain in the distance, then the sound of running footsteps, followed at last by a longer cry, this time of despair. Staples had plunged into a sinkhole in his desperate attempt to get away, ignoring the warning flare of his charm. We heard the sound of struggling after that, but although we followed as quickly as possible under the circumstances, we could not be certain precisely where the sound had originated.

His body was not recovered until the following day and even then only after a great deal of difficulty. But the threat to Sir Henry Baskerville had ended.

CHAPTER TWENTY TWO

Wanda tied up the loose ends before Captain Lester took his leave. Dennis Staples was the quite legitimate son of Arthur Staples, who had died in Haiti without ever telling the rest of the family that he had married and given birth to a son. Perhaps it never occurred to him that Dennis might someday be in line for the family fortune. One small irony is that if Dennis had declared himself, Sir Henry would almost certainly have welcomed him and given him a generous allowance, and being slightly younger, Dennis might well have someday inherited everything quite legitimately.

We will never know exactly how it came about that Selden died, but Dolores told us that the griffin had escaped at least once before. The magical compulsion that forced it to obey her husband was not as effective in his absence. Shortly before the attack on Charles Baskerville, it had broken through the rather flimsy bulkhead door, which had not even been locked, and which had recently been replaced with a tarpaulin. Dennis had been in a terrible state until it eventually returned of its own accord, having grown used to having food available without the necessity to hunt and kill its own. It is likely that something similar happened again and that Selden was no more than collateral damage. If the griffin escaped again, it might well have been drawn to the scent on the clothing Mrs. Lionel had innocently provided to her brother. We refrained from explaining this to her in order to spare her any additional grief.

Dolores did indeed send the warning note to Sir Henry at the hotel. She insisted at her trial that she had never wanted to be involved with her husband's plans but had been terrified of disobeying him. There may have been some element of truth in this, but it is likely fear of discovery was the true motive.

Dolores also confirmed that her husband planned to move away once Sir Henry was disposed of. He had already established himself under his real name in Providence, and intended to conduct his claim against the estate entirely through his attorneys, without ever returning to the valley. He wore a false beard and lifts in his shoes when he was in Providence, just as a precaution, and it was in this guise that he followed Sir Henry during his Boston stay.

I should also mention that Sir Henry did in fact marry Lydia Longtree, and so far as is known, they are a happy couple. I still have my suspicions about her motives, but so long as she convinces her new husband that she feels genuine affection for him, then I suppose there is no harm done.

Liz Lawrence has also been married, to one of her customers, the son of a farmer who has no affinity for the land and who much prefers the life of a tavern keeper. His family has loaned them the money to build an extension of the building so that they will have six rooms to rent. I wish them the best of luck. Her former tormentor, Randolph Doyle, is currently serving a twenty year term after being convicted on sixteen of thirty-four charges of corruption. I doubt she will be bothered by him again.

And finally there is Wanda and myself. We're back in Boston and the caseload has dropped off again. My temporary title of assistant has not been mentioned since our return, but I received a very nice bonus for my work on the case – Sir Henry had been very generous when he settled his bill – and Julia has upgraded our vacation plans accordingly.

As to Wanda, well, Wanda keeps her own council. And waits for the next interesting case.

The end...

...but Wanda will return in *Ten Little Homunculi*.

www.ingramcontent.com/pod-product-compliance
Lightning Source LLC
Chambersburg PA
CBHW071939170626
46813CB00005B/1789